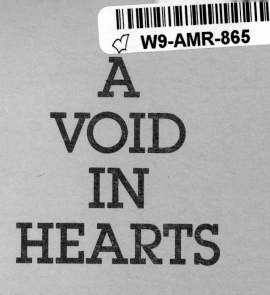

# A VOID IN HEARTS

## A Brady Coyne Mystery

## William G. Tapply

BALLANTINE BOOKS • NEW YORK

Library of Congress Catalog Card Number: 88-12203

ISBN 0-345-35868-6

This edition published by arrangement with Charles Scribner's Sons,
an Imprint of Macmillan Publishing Company.

Manufactured in the United States of America

First Ballantine Books Edition: March 1990

Also by William G. Tapply
*Published by Ballantine Books:*

THE VULGAR BOATMAN

DEAD MEAT

THE MARINE CORPSE

FOLLOW THE SHARKS

THE DUTCH BLUE ERROR

DEATH AT CHARITY'S POINT

*For Mike and Wendy McGill*

# 1

Les Katz peered at me with his dirt-colored eyes. "It has occurred to me," he said slowly, "that I may have committed a crime."

I glanced around. The restaurant was empty of other patrons, not that surprising at three on a Thursday afternoon in January at Hung Moon's in Somerville, Massachusetts. Two waitresses—they looked Vietnamese to me—sat at a table across the room under a plastic fern, watching us. I knew if I lifted a finger or arched an eyebrow I would be offered an hour of exquisite oriental pleasure at reasonable rates. I was not tempted.

Les spent a lot of time at Hung Moon's. "I'm addicted to MSG," he once told me. "Also, there's this chick named Soo Ling who's got a tongue like an anaconda."

Les Katz was a private investigator whom I used on those relatively rare occasions when I needed one. My law practice consists mostly of estates and contracts, the mundane paper stuff that my wealthy clients need. Now and then, however, a client asks me for services that I don't perform myself, and that's when I call Les. Once, for example, he found the fourteen-year-old daughter of a State Street banker in the back room of a Combat Zone bar for me, and he took her back to the private school in Weston where her estranged parents had placed her for safekeeping. Another time Les nailed an engineer who was selling company secrets to a competitor.

Les was very good at his work. He had never failed me. This made me a hero in the eyes of my clients and Les a hero of sorts in mine.

He was a brown-and-gray man, distinguished by his non-descriptness. Medium height, medium build, medium middle-aged, neither attractive nor ugly, he blended in. He was blessed, moreover, with a seemingly limitless supply of patience. "How," I once asked him, "can you sit in a car all night staring into the dark? How can you spend weeks on end twirling on a barstool?"

"Simple," he said. "I play old bridge hands in my head. The real secret is to drink Coke, not booze. A slow, steady intake of caffeine. We Sam Spade types gotta be alert, you know. Danger lurks behind every door, and all that shit. What I don't understand is how you can devote a career to shuffling manila folders and changing commas into semicolons. I mean, how many times can a man write 'party of the first part' on yellow legal pads before he begins to claw at his own eyeballs?"

Now he was leaning across the damp table at me, a glass of Coca-Cola in front of him, a half smile on his forgettable face. After a moment he removed his cigar from his mouth and jabbed at me with its soggy end. "Did you hear me?" he said. "About me maybe committing a crime?"

"I heard you, Les."

"Well?"

I shrugged. He frowned. Then he said, "Oh, right." He extracted his wallet from his hip pocket, removed a bill, folded it once the long way, and extended it to me between two fingers. I took it and smoothed it out.

"A ten spot," I observed. "Something heavy, Les?"

"Are we . . . ?"

I took a ballpoint pen from my pocket and scribbled on a napkin. I pushed it across the table. Les glanced at it, wrote his name on it, and pushed it back to me. I folded it and stuck it into my shirt pocket.

"Now," I said, "I am officially and legally retained. You are my privileged client. I am your lawyer."

"I can talk?"

"Freely. Liberally. Talk dirty if you want."

"It's a little embarrassing."

"It usually is."

"Actually, it's not as sordid as it may sound."

I lit a cigarette. "You figure you're getting your money's worth out of this, Les?"

"Okay," he said. He clamped down on his cigar and fired it up. "You've got the meter running, huh?"

"Spit it out."

He nodded and leaned toward me. "Good-looking lady comes to your office, wants you to get the goods on her old man, who she thinks is scraping his carrot somewhere else. What do you conclude?"

"I conclude," I said, "that maybe this good-looking lady's shagging somebody on the side, wants a little insurance in case her old man hires an investigator to check her out."

"I thought of that," said Les. "The other thing I thought of, though, is maybe this good-looking lady's got something wrong with her, her old man needs to play around. Two sides to every story, right?"

"Everybody plays around," I observed.

Les cocked his head at me. "That ain't true."

"Okay. I stand corrected. People who aren't married, you don't call it playing around. Anyway, so what?"

"So this lady is telling me she thinks the guy is finding some interesting new place to dip his wick, and she's looking at me through these eyes that make you want to jump right in. Slim, tall, all this blond hair. She looked like that actress there. Farrah Fawcett. Had this voice, made you feel like you just finished having sex with her to hear her talk. Brady, I'm telling you, she was absolutely gorgeous. Anyway, I tell her, sure, that's what I do for a living. I ask her a few questions, trying to get a line on the guy. She's acting typical. Last thing she wants is the guy finding out she's sicced a gumshoe onto him. She's nervous. Like she wants to know, but doesn't, too. Pays in cash. Don't try to call her. Don't go near their house. Anyway, to make a long story short—"

"It's a little late for that, Les."

He frowned at me. "Huh?"

"It's already a long story."

"Right. I follow the guy. Sure enough. She's right. Nooners. Superdiscreet. Twice a week, but different days, always they meet in a different place. Once she's in a taxi that stops on the corner for him. Another time they have lunch at separate tables at the Oyster House and he follows her out, they go to a hotel in Brookline. Once he sits beside her on a bench on the Common, they don't go anywhere. Just lean close to each other and talk. I got my trusty three-hundred-millimeter lens working. Still, nothing definitive, you know?"

I nodded.

"Okay," he continued. "So I follow them for three weeks. They've got a thing going, no doubt in my mind. But damned if I could get what I needed. And you know I'm good at what I do."

"Photos. Tapes. *In flagrante delicto.* You got nothing juicy."

"Right. I never knew where they were going until they got there. I had the feeling that she was running the show, making the arrangements. She's done this before, you ask me. So there I am. The old lady, she's gonna call me, find out what I got. What do I say? I think her old man's messing around, all right. I can show her a picture of the alienator of her husband's affections. But no evidence of anything. In other words, I haven't earned my money."

"For all you can tell, these are business meetings," I said.

"Hell, Brady, I know they ain't business meetings. I know exactly what they are. But these two've got me stumped. I admit it. Funny thing, though. I started thinking, this guy keeps meeting this lady, they've obviously got something going, and next thing I know I start to feel sorry for them. They've gotta sneak around, and this lady, she's not all that attractive, so I begin to think they're really in love or something. More than just, you know, good, healthy hormones run amok. They've got something nice, it seems to me, and who am I to interfere?''

"Come off it, Les."

"No, really. I actually began to feel guilty."

I shook my head slowly. "Why don't you buy us another drink."

"Capital idea." He glanced over at the two Vietnamese waitresses and nodded. They discussed it for a moment and then one of them came toward us. Her skirt was so tight that she walked as if her feet were bound, little birdlike steps, one foot precisely in front of the other.

"Gennumun?" she said, an expectant smile on her rosebud lips.

"Another," said Les, gesturing to our empty glasses. "Bourbon for my uncle. Coke for me."

The girl glanced over her shoulder at her friend at the table across the room. They exchanged small shrugs before she tiptoed away.

"So," resumed Les, examining the dead end of his cigar, "I thought about it for a while. Finally I realized what I had to do."

"Les—"

"No, listen. My heart was in absolutely the right place. I call the guy up at his office. Tell him my name, my job, and ask him if he'd like to meet with me. He sounds very shook up. Naturally. So I meet him at this grungy bar in Chelsea, for God's sake. His choice. We sit in a booth. He refuses a drink. I tell him, I say I've been following him for three weeks, I know what he's doing. I've got photos of him and the lady. I tell him I got nothing really incriminating, but he probably still wouldn't want his wife to see them. He agrees instantly. I tell him, who am I to butt into his life? He seems to agree with that, too. Then you know what he did?''

"He offered to buy the pictures from you," I said.

Les sat back and placed both of his hands flat on the table. "How did you figure that out?"

"I think you left the little hints you might have let slip out of your narrative, Les. You did suggest to this man, in a very circuitous way, I'm sure, that if he had the photos, then you wouldn't have them to show his wife. Am I right?"

"Well," he said, his eyes slipping away from mine, "maybe I did. Not that I really intended to, understand, and not that I necessarily went there with that in my mind. I am not a devious man, Brady."

"Ho, ho," I said.

Les shrugged. "Anyway, he wanted the photos real bad. See, I said to myself, Les, I said, you give the wife these pictures, all it's gonna do is make everybody unhappy. She can't use them to divorce the guy and take him to the cleaners, because they're just not explicit enough. So she gets nothing out of it. But she's miserable, even so, and she makes things miserable for the poor guy. But if he gets the pictures—see, Brady, they just show the two of them getting out of a cab together, walking into a hotel, sitting beside each other on a park bench—if he has them, that way nobody gets hurt."

The waitress brought our drinks and scurried back to her friend across the room. I removed the paper parasol from mine and sipped. Cheap bourbon. I put the drink down, lit a Winston, and studied Les.

"You're thinking bad thoughts," he said.

"It's blackmail, Les. Legal opinion."

"I knew you'd say that."

"Unethical. Illegal. Is that what you paid me ten bucks to tell you?"

"I do feel a lot better, telling you all this."

"Convert, then. Priests don't charge anything for hearing confessions. You going to tell me the rest of it?"

He frowned at his cigar. Then he smashed it into the ashtray. "The wife called me. That was how we had left it. She'd get in touch. Didn't want me calling her."

"What'd you tell her?"

He smiled apologetically and lifted his hands palms outward, as if it were self-evident. "I told her I had nothing on the man and as far as I could tell I wouldn't be able to get anything. I told her to forget it. I told her I couldn't help her. I told her our slate was clean. She had given me a retainer and expenses for three weeks. Cash on the spot when she hired me. And that was that. End of story."

"A happy ending, then."

"You think so?"

"Are you worried?"

He shook his head doubtfully. "Nope. Guess not. I'm clear, huh?"

"What could happen?"

He sighed loudly. "I've been trying to figure it out. She could tell him she hired me, right? How relieved she is that he's still the faithful spouse. But hell, he knows this already. Nothing new to him. No problem to me. Now, he sure as hell isn't gonna tell her that he bought these photos from some creepy private dick that show him with this broad he's banging, and if he does, the last thing on her mind is my, ah, dubious ethics. So nothing can happen."

I studied the half-empty glass of bourbon that sat in front of me. There was a large black speck frozen in the middle of one of the ice cubes. It could have been a cigarette ash. Or a bug. "Les," I said evenly, "you extorted money from a man. You lied to your client. You took money from both of them. You are a disgrace. Another legal opinion."

"I know, I know. But I think I did the right thing."

"You're a social worker, maybe you did the right thing. You're a private investigator, you plain fucked up."

"So what do you think I should do?"

I grinned. "You should give the guy his money back. You should go to the wife and tell her what you found out. You can't play God in people's lives, and you can't blackmail folks." I leaned forward, my elbows planted on the table, my chin on my fists. "By the way," I said, "didn't the man ask for negatives?"

"Oh, sure he did."

"And did you give them to him?"

"I hate to tell you this."

"So don't. I rendered you more than ten bucks' worth already." I pushed my chair back and started to stand.

He reached across the table and put his hand on my wrist. "No, wait. You want another ten-spot?"

I sat down. "The hell with it. What about the negatives?"

"You're not going to like this."

I shrugged.

"I had a set of negatives with me. We burned them."

"We?"

"Well, actually I burned them. In the ashtray on the table in that cruddy bar in Chelsea."

"What negatives were they, Les?"

He rolled his brown eyes upward. He reminded me of a sheep. His expression certainly qualified as sheepish. "It was a roll of film I shot last summer on the Cape. Nothing much good. Artsy stuff. Boats. Sand dunes. Surf. Not my forte."

"And the man didn't examine them?"

"I kinda did it quick. Talked through it. He never questioned it."

"You are a piece of work, you know that?"

Les smiled. "What can I say?"

"You still have the negatives, then."

"Yep. I got 'em."

"So what are you going to do?"

He shrugged elaborately. "What can I do?"

"You can make another set of prints, show them to your client. You can give the poor guy his money back."

Les stared over at the two waitresses. One of them waggled her fingers at him. He waggled back at her. She opened her mouth and ran her tongue all the way around the inside of her lips. Les smiled and turned to me. "Nah. I don't think so. But thanks for the advice. It was worth ten bucks. Easy."

# 2

A brilliant January sun had burned away the smog and crud that usually hung over the city. I kept swiveling around in my chair to look at it. The fishing season was too far off to allow myself to dream about it. The golf courses would remain frozen for months. I liked the gray days of January better, when slush lay in puddles on the sidewalks and the dirty snow huddled miserably against the buildings, and a man could more easily accept the futility of wishing for spring.

Anyway, I had contracts to revise, estates to settle, codicils to compose, clients to call. There might be the odd divorce, perhaps a deed to research. I would get through this day, and the next.

There came the scratching of long, well-tended fingernails on my door. I called, "Come on in, Julie."

My dark-haired, green-eyed secretary entered, with a smile that eclipsed the brilliance of the sun, and a mug of coffee, freshly brewed. She placed the mug on my desk and herself on the chair beside it.

"We have a problem," she said.

"Keeping our passions in check," I answered.

"Not that one. That is not a problem."

"Speak for yourself."

"I emphatically was. This concerns our telephone system."

I sipped my coffee and lit a cigarette. "Sounds like just the kind of problem I'd like to tackle today. Shoot."

"Okay." She took a deep breath. "When we put somebody on hold, because you're making plans to go fishing with Mr. McDevitt or Dr. Adams or somebody, like the time you were arranging that trip to Alaska, and Dr. Adams wanted to bring his wife and you really didn't want a woman along but you couldn't figure out how to tell him and besides you've got this little thing for her anyway, and while you were beating around the bush with your friend, Mrs. Bailey had to wait for nearly twenty minutes to tell you that they were taking her husband off life support—"

"Jesus, Julie. Get to it."

She scowled. "I am. Anyway, you do spend a lot of time on the phone."

"So I do. The telephone is an indispensable tool for attorneys."

She gave me a phony smile. "You bet. Listen. What we can do, they say, is, we can have music play into the phone while somebody's on hold."

I nodded. "Good. Sounds good."

"Well, the question is, what music? I don't know about you, but that Ray Conniff stuff makes me feel like I'm on an elevator and want to get off. No way I'd stay on hold if they played that crap into my ear. So what kind of music do you want?"

"Mötley Crüe. Twisted Sister. Ozzy Osbourne."

"Get serious, Brady."

"Okay," I said. I frowned for her so she'd know I was giving this conundrum my full attention. I swiveled around to study the Copley Square skyline. Then I swiveled back. "For my clientele, I think Benny Goodman, Tommy Dorsey, maybe a little Sinatra."

"Don't you think that stuff is a little avant-garde for your clients?"

I nodded. "Good point. They do tend to be pretty old and conservative. What about Bach, then?"

"I don't know," she said. "All that weird counterpoint. Unsettling for old nerves."

"Mozart?"

"Hmmm," she said, pretending to cogitate on the matter. "Maybe Ray Conniff isn't such a bad idea after all."

The light on my desk phone blinked. Julie reached over and picked it up. "Brady L. Coyne, attorney at law," she said into it. "Good morning."

She paused, then smiled, first at the phone and then at me. "Well, I'm trying to get him to do a little work for a change. Not having much luck, actually. . . . Sure. I'm sure he'll be happy to. Hang on a sec."

Julie held her hand over the receiver. "It's Gloria."

My former wife called me at least weekly. Julie considered all of Gloria's calls urgent. Julie believed—not without some justification—that my relationship with Gloria had not been entirely resolved by our divorce eight years earlier. She hoped we would, as she persisted in saying, "get back together."

Gloria had raised our two sons, Billy and Joey—William and Joseph, Gloria usually called them—through all the tough times. She never accused me of evading my responsibilities. She didn't have to, because I slogged around in my own guilt without any encouragement. Usually when she called me it was with a problem. A balky oil burner. Squirrels in the attic of the house in Wellesley that I moved out of when we split. Billy's physics grade. Joey's experimentation with cannabis.

There were other agendas between us that remained unstated. I was sure she was as aware of them as I. Never either during or after our rocky marriage had either of us declared an end to love. It was a subject that, by tacit agreement, remained taboo.

I took the phone from Julie. She winked at me and left the office, closing the door behind her.

"Hi, hon," I said into the phone, using a term that had once been an endearment and remained as a habit.

"Brady," said Gloria, "do you know what today is?"

"Um, Friday. January something-or-other."

"Try again."

"Well, it's not Groundhog Day, I know that, because Groundhog Day is my favorite holiday and I've got it circled on my calendar. That doesn't come up until next month. And we just had Martin Luther King Day. Oh, shit. Did I forget somebody's birthday?"

"Nobody that I know of. One of your Hungarian ladies, maybe."

"There's only one Hungarian lady, Gloria. It's not her birthday. Give me a hint."

"Something important happened in your life on this date several years ago."

"I passed the bar exam. No, that was in August. I remember, because I had just gotten back from Montana and—"

"Brady, I'm serious."

"I give up, Gloria."

"It's our anniversary, damn you."

"Aha!" I said. "If this is a test, you can't nail me with trick questions. We got married in May. I missed a whole week of trout fishing because of our honeymoon trip to that little tropical island where I got a sunburn surfcasting and there were twin beds in our room."

"Not of our wedding. Our divorce, dummy."

I sighed. "Oh. Right. I had forgotten the exact date."

"Do you remember the day?" Gloria's voice was soft.

"Indeed. A memorable day. A significant day. I wasn't aware that we acknowledged this day as some sort of holiday. We haven't exactly celebrated it. We never exchanged cards, sent flowers—"

"Well, I was thinking that we should."

"Send flowers?"

"Celebrate it. Or acknowledge it. Consider it an important day."

"Well, then, happy anniversary of our divorce, Gloria, and many more."

"Don't be facile, Brady Coyne."

"I'm sorry."

She chuckled. "You used to say that a lot."

"I had a lot to be sorry about. I was not a very good husband."

"To me, you weren't. But that was mostly me. You were okay."

"What is this, Gloria?"

"I thought we should celebrate. That's all." She paused. There was apology in her voice.

"Why?"

"Do you remember what we did that day?"

There had been no animosity, I remembered that. We had walked out of the courthouse with our lawyers. On the sidewalk out front, while rain misted down and glazed the street, our attorneys shook hands all around and walked away. Gloria and I remained standing there, reluctant, for some reason, to make the final parting.

"Well," I had said.

Gloria's smile was small. "Well."

"I guess that's it, then."

"It's not like we won't be seeing each other," she said. "The boys. You'll be around."

"Of course."

"I bet there are a lot of things we have forgotten about."

"I did leave some books I want at the house."

"Sure. Just come by anytime."

"And look, hon. If money is ever a problem . . ."

She nodded quickly. "It's a generous settlement. You were very kind."

"It wasn't like it was really adversarial, after all."

"No."

Suddenly we became awkward. I lit a cigarette. Something to do. Gloria looked at her watch. She smiled brightly up at me. "Well, the single woman has no plans for lunch."

I hunched into my topcoat. "The single lawyer with no lunch date, either."

We went to the Iruña, a little Spanish place just off Harvard Square. We had a fruity red wine, clicked glasses, and agreed that it was a silly thing for us to do. Gloria ordered an avocado stuffed with seafood. I had a bowl of paella. We sampled from each other's spoon. We finished the bottle of wine. Then we went to my car and—on what pretext I can't recall—drove to my new little studio apartment on Beacon Street.

We made love on the rented pullout sofa, and afterward Gloria cried and I held her familiar body close and promised I'd never abandon her. And when we made love the second time, it was as if it had never happened before. I found new hollows along her back, a different roundness to her belly, a startling hunger in her mouth.

We both recognized it. We knew we had lost something that we could never recover. We were saying good-bye. It wasn't easy.

And since that day we had kept our awkward distance from each other. We avoided being alone together. The telephone connected us. Sometimes we went places with the boys. We met at parties, funerals, graduations. We acknowledged that we liked each other. Sometimes the line got blurry. Usually it was I who drew it sharp again.

"I remember the day very well, hon. It was a long time ago."

"Eight years. Exactly."

"A lot has changed."

"Yes. It has. I was thinking . . ."

"I don't think it's a good idea."

"The Iruña is still there," she said quickly. "It would be—"

"It would be dumb."

I didn't recognize the sound I heard. It was muffled. It took me a moment to realize that she had covered the receiver. It was a sigh of exasperation. Or anger. Or it might have been a sob.

"Look, Gloria."

"You are a first-class prick, Brady Coyne. All I wanted to do was have a civilized lunch with a man I like. An old friend. And you, you're thinking we're still where we were eight years ago." She blew out her breath quickly. It hissed in my ear. It reminded me of the natural-childbirth classes we had taken together before Billy was born. "I don't know about you, but I'm in a different place now. And if you can't handle it, well—"

"Hey," I said. "Whoa. You're right. I spoke without thinking."

"The Iruña at noon, then," she said.

"You're bullying me, Gloria."

"For a change."

I laughed. "Okay. What the hell. Maybe we should go easy on the wine this time, though."

"Maybe," she said softly, "we shouldn't."

I replaced the receiver gently and leaned back in my chair, my fingers laced together behind my head. It would be dumb, I had said, I was right. Picking at old scabs that had been hardening for eight years. Dumb.

I sighed. I would be jovial, distant. I would creep carefully around the sores that still festered. Delay, misdirection, evasion. Good lawyer's tricks. I could handle it.

The telephone buzzed. I picked it up. "Yes, Julie?"

"You've got a call. She's been holding. We should've had music for her."

"Who is it?"

"Rebecca Katz?" It was a question.

"I don't know her."

"Well, that's all I can tell you. Maybe someone you picked up on Washington Street."

"I don't lurk around Washington Street, Julie."

"She sounds agitated. I'll put her through."

There was a click. I said into the phone, "This is Brady Coyne."

"Mr. Coyne, this is Becca Katz."

I hesitated. "Yes?"

"Lester's wife."

"Oh, sure. What can I do for you?"

"The other day Les mentioned that he had retained you. You're his lawyer?"

Les had given me ten dollars. I had given him advice. It was not my usual business arrangement. "Yes," I told his wife. "What's up?"

"He wants to speak to you. You're the only one he'll talk to. He's—"

"So put him on, Mrs. Katz."

There was a long pause. When she finally spoke, I detected a tension in her voice that I hadn't noticed before. "I can't put him on, Mr. Coyne."

"Well . . ."

"I'm at the hospital. Les was unconscious for around thirty hours. He just came out of it. He asked for you. 'Brady,' he said. 'Gotta talk to Brady.' The policeman came in. Les wouldn't talk to him. He wouldn't talk to me. 'Get me Brady,' he said. That would be you, wouldn't it?"

"Jesus, Mrs. Katz. What happened?"

"Hit-and-run. Right in front of our house. Wednesday night. Actually, Thursday morning. He had been working. Just gotten home. He's—his skull is fractured. Pelvis broken. Lots of internal damage. Bleeding. They don't know. They did some kind of emergency operation. He's been too critical for them to do much else. He wants you. Can you come?"

"Of course," I said. "What hospital?"

"Mass General. Please. Hurry."

"I'm on my way."

I grabbed my topcoat. "I have to go over to Mass General," I told Julie on my way out.

"What about our problem?"

"Huh?"

"The music."

"You were right. Ray Conniff. It's what people expect."

# 3

A cab took me over to Mass General. By the time I had negotiated lobbies, elevators, and corridors and found the intensive-care unit, nearly an hour had passed from the time of Becca Katz's call.

A nurse sat behind a barricade, facing a bank of computer monitors. Dots and lines bounded across the screens, beeping and humming rhythmically. She had her head down, studying some papers. She had thick wrists. She wore no rings on her fingers.

I cleared my throat. She ignored me.

"Excuse me," I said.

She looked up. Her face was surprisingly young and delicate. "Yes?"

"My name if Coyne. I'm looking for Lester Katz."

A hand touched my shoulder. I turned. A policeman was standing there. "You're Coyne?"

"Yes. Mrs. Katz called me."

He steered me away from the nurses' station with a gentle hand on my elbow. I caught the nurse's eye for an instant. She gave me a small shake of her head.

In a corner were arranged two small sofas, upholstered florally. A square table held scattered copies of old *Newsweek* magazines. I sat with the policeman.

"I'm Kerrigan," he said. "I was the first one at the scene."

"Les . . . ?"

He shook his head. "He died about fifteen minutes ago. I'm sorry."

I fumbled for a cigarette, a reflex. Kerrigan touched my arm and pointed to a No Smoking sign. I shrugged and put the pack back into my pocket. "What happened?" I said.

"He was conscious for only a couple of minutes. Asked for you. That was it. Blood clots in his brain. The doctors said it was inevitable. Nothing they could do."

"Shit," I mumbled.

Officer Kerrigan had thick, curly red hair and a skimpy mustache of a slightly darker shade. He had startling blue eyes, round and clear as a baby's. He was a young man. To me, he looked like a teenager. He was probably twenty-five. A patch on his uniform read "Somerville Police."

"Where's Mrs. Katz?" I said.

"A doctor took her somewhere. I suppose there are papers to be signed. Authorization for an autopsy. Permission to take his organs, maybe." He shrugged.

"She told me it was hit-and-run."

He nodded. "I got the call. Two fifty-four a.m. Took me only a minute or two to get there. Weird scene. Middle of the night, dead of winter, just the two of them there in the street."

"Her and Les?"

He ran his forefinger over his mustache, as if it were new and he wasn't used to it. "She was the one who called it in. Then she went out, put a blanket over him. She's sitting there on the street holding his head in her lap, getting blood all over her like Jackie Kennedy, there. He was a mess, Mr. Coyne. I never saw anything like it. I've talked to some of the other guys. They say you get used to it, but I don't know."

He looked up, appealing to me. "I just came on the force a few months ago. They don't prepare you for this in school."

"Did she see it happen?"

"She said she was in bed but not asleep. He was working. A private detective, you know. Worked odd hours, I guess. She said she never slept until he came home. Said she heard the thump. The car hitting him. That was the first thing she heard."

"No horn, no squeal of brakes?"

He shook his head. "No. Of course, she may not be that reliable. She's been pretty upset. She might've been dozing when it happened. But she doesn't remember any other sound. Just that thump."

"Then what?" I said gently as Kerrigan's eyes wavered.

"Then she called the police. Then she threw on a robe, grabbed a blanket, and ran out there. I was there in a couple of minutes, like I said, and the ambulance came right along. Brought him here. She came in the ambulance. I followed in my cruiser a little later."

"And you've been here ever since?"

He nodded. "I cleared it. Figured, if he came to I could talk to him. See what I could learn from his wife. The chief said it was a good idea."

"And you cared."

He smiled. "Doing my job."

"Right. So you figure this was a routine hit-and-run?"

"Routine?"

I waved my hand. "So to speak."

"Well, it's obviously a hit-and-run. Somebody hit him and kept going. I'm not sure what's routine. Why? You got a different idea?"

I hesitated. "No. Not really."

"What do you mean, not really?"

"Nothing. I don't have a different idea. So how do you reconstruct what happened?"

Kerrigan sat back. I had gentled him onto more familiar ground, the abstractions of tape-measured distances, estimates of speed and time, profiles of bodies chalked onto pavement, names and addresses of witnesses. Forensic detail. The humdrum, mundane stuff that allows men who must confront death to deal with it.

"Mr. Katz parked on the north side of Chestnut Street, across from his house. He was just starting to cross when he was hit by a car traveling east. He was thrown forward and sideward against another parked car. It was right under a streetlight. The road had some icy patches on it, but basically it was clear. No skid marks. As near as we could reconstruct it, the car caught him at the hips. Smashed his pelvis, ruptured his spleen, and God knows what else. Lots of internal damage, I guess. Had all kinds of tubes going in and out of him. Then when he hit the parked car it fractured his skull. They operated on his spleen, which saved his life for a short time. I guess there was so much swelling in his brain that they couldn't do much except drill some holes and hope for the best. The doctor said it was like a miracle he had that couple of minutes of consciousness. When he asked for you." Kerrigan regarded me solemnly with those innocent blue eyes. "Why would he ask for you, Mr. Coyne?"

"Well," I began. And then I stopped. I was about to tell Kerrigan about my conversation with Les at Hung Moon's restaurant. As the story flitted through my mind, I realized it sounded irrelevant. "Well," I repeated, "I was his lawyer. And we were friends. Who knows what was going through his mind in the condition he was in."

Kerrigan stared at me for a moment, then nodded. "Yeah. I guess."

"Why would Les park across the street, do you suppose?" I asked, just to divert the policeman from inquiring further into my relationship with Les.

"I asked Mrs. Katz that. She said that he kept odd hours, and the others who live in the building—it's a four-family house—they'd get parked in if he used the driveway. There's parking on one side only on that street in the winter."

"You're sure he was getting out of his car, not on his way to get in?"

"That's what she said. She said he was coming home."

"Did she know where he'd been?"

He shook his head. "She said she didn't know that much about his work. He had jobs. Following people. You know what he did. She said she didn't like what he did, didn't want to know about it. Do you think it matters?"

I shrugged. "I don't know."

"If there's something we should know, Mr. Coyne . . ."

"If I think of anything, I'll let you know."

Kerrigan narrowed his eyes. It matured him instantly. "You think Mr. Katz was murdered, don't you?"

"I think it's possible, someone in his line of work. Bound to have enemies."

He nodded. "I think it's possible, too. Someone hits someone by accident, their first instinct is to stop. Even if they're drunk, they'll hit the brakes. Driving away, that's a conscious decision, not a reaction. The thing is, Mrs. Katz didn't hear anything that would indicate a car had stopped and then started up again. She said she jumped right out of bed and went to the window. Got there within seconds of hearing that godawful thump. She didn't see a car. Not even a flash of taillights. This guy didn't even slow down." He shrugged. "I'm new at this. But I've been thinking a lot about it over the past thirty-six hours. I've been thinking about nothing else."

I took a deep breath. I desperately wanted a cigarette. "Look," I said. "Les blackmailed somebody earlier this week."

Kerrigan's eyebrows arched. "Who?"

"I don't know." I summarized my conversation with Les. When I was done, Kerrigan sighed. "It's not much, is it?"

"It's something."

"I'm not exactly in a position to spend a lot of time on this." He flapped his hands in apology. "We've got no witnesses at all. There was just that thump. Not enough to wake anybody up. Even when the ambulance got there, nobody came out of their house. I've talked with the lieutenant a couple of times since I've been here. He says, something like this, usually a guy has a chance to think about it, sober up, he turns himself in. Or somebody else does. They see the dent in his car, they hear what happened, they know the guy was out late, came home drunk. Or there was somebody in the car with him, doesn't want to get in trouble. So they give the cops an anonymous call. Point is, Mr. Coyne, investigations sound nice. All that fancy television stuff, with computers and whatnot. But what gets crimes solved most of the time is somebody telling on somebody else, or somebody turning themselves in. So the message I'm getting here is, I've done a nice job, done about all I can do, but with no witnesses, no kind of evidence at all, it's time to get on with things." He turned down the corners of his mouth and arched his eyebrows.

"What I just told you," I said. "That changes things, doesn't it?"

He smiled doubtfully. "I'll run it past the lieutenant. If you had a name . . ."

"Maybe I can come up with it."

Kerrigan glanced past my shoulder. "Oh, oh," he said.

I turned. A doctor was standing by the nurse's station, leaning back with an elbow cocked up on the counter. He was talking to a woman. "Rebecca Katz?" I said.

Kerrigan nodded.

She was short and slender, with a boyish haircut. She was looking up at the doctor as he talked, nodding and flashing perfunctory smiles. The doctor made a gesture with his hand, and she watched it move, as if it held a weapon.

After a moment, the doctor straightened, touched her shoulder lightly, turned, and moved behind the counter, where he bent and conferred with the thick-wristed nurse. Rebecca Katz looked around. Her eyes settled on me and Kerrigan.

Kerrigan stood up and beckoned to her. I stood also, and she came toward us.

She went directly to Kerrigan, ignoring me. "Well, that's it," she said to him. She had a husky voice for such a small body. Up close, I noticed the lines etched onto her face and the streaks of gray in her sandy hair.

"This is Mr. Coyne," said Kerrigan.

"Oh," she said. "I'm sorry. I thought you were another policeman. Officer Kerrigan has been such a big help." She held out her hand to me. "I'm happy to meet Lester's attorney. I hope you'll—"

I took her hand. It felt cool and small in mine. "Of course," I said. "Whatever I can do."

You'll get your ten bucks' worth, Les, old pal, I said to myself. Pro bono work had never been a priority of mine. But this new widow would need an attorney, and it looked like she thought I was it. This was certainly no time to disabuse her.

The three of us stood there awkwardly for a few moments. Finally Kerrigan said, "Well, I've got to get going. If you remember anything else about the other night, Mrs. Katz . . ."

She nodded. "Sure."

"Call me."

"I will."

Kerrigan shook hands with both of us and left. Rebecca Katz and I remained standing uncomfortably, watching him go. We turned to each other at the same instant. She said, "Well" at the same time I said, "Um . . ." We laughed quickly.

"Thank you for coming," she said. She ran her fingers through her hair. "Oh, I am a mess. I haven't slept. It's—I haven't realized it yet, I know. Everything happened so suddenly. It's like I've been watching myself through the wrong end of a telescope. Do you understand?"

"I think so," I said. "Would you like to get some coffee?"

"Actually, I'd like to eat something. The nurses have been very kind. But I haven't been very hungry." She shook her head. "Suddenly I'm famished."

The nurse directed us to the cafeteria—down the corridor to the end, go right to the elevators, down to the lobby, take a sharp left . . .

She chatted compulsively along the way. The doctors had

been so honest with her, the nurses so thoughtful, the chair she dozed in so uncomfortable. I murmured at the right places. If it hadn't been for the way she kept digging her fingernails into the palms of her hands, she might have fooled me. That plus the fact that she avoided mention of Les.

I got a salad in a plastic-topped container with a little aluminum foil envelope of Thousand Island dressing and a cup of coffee. Becca took a chicken salad sandwich and tea. We transported them on tin trays to a corner table.

Doctors and nurses dominated a group of tables near the middle of the large cafeteria. They talked loudly and laughed often and were constantly coming and going. A bored female voice summoned them periodically over an invisible speaker. Here and there around the perimeter huddled citizens like Becca and me, mostly in pairs, picking absentmindedly at their food and whispering solemnly. They seemed to be waiting for bad news to find them.

I squeezed the dressing onto my salad. Becca tore the cellophane off her sandwich. She lifted it to her mouth, hesitated, then put it down. She said, "Dammit." Tears welled up in her eyes and then spilled out. She neither wiped them away nor covered her face. She cried silently but without self-consciousness, and when I started to move to her, she gestured to me to stay where I was.

It probably didn't last more than a minute. To me it seemed much longer. Then she fumbled a tissue from her bag and wiped her face.

She smiled wanly at me. "That's been coming on for a while. Sorry."

"You're lucky you can cry. It's supposed to make you feel better."

"I'll do it some more, no doubt." She bit into her sandwich. "This is delicious," she mumbled.

She wolfed down her sandwich while I ate my salad and watched her. She had once been beautiful, and perhaps she would be again. But time—or tragedy—had marked her, sucking the life from her skin and cobwebbing an intricate pattern of tiny lines onto her face. Tendons rose starkly from the backs of her hands. I wondered how she'd look after a good night's sleep.

"We didn't have a very good marriage," she said abruptly. "I think Les was being kind to me by marrying me. I loved him in my simple, naive way, this brilliant, bizarre man. He was older than me. Experienced. Well traveled. Everything that I wasn't. He had been married once before. Lester was not a conventional man. He liked to make his own rules. I never really got to understand him. At first it didn't matter. Then it mattered desperately to me. He didn't care. He never tried to help me. Oh, I think he cared for me. Or cared about me. But I didn't really matter to him. I just wasn't important. He knew how I felt about his—his eavesdropping, his skulking and sneaking and spying. I despised it. He didn't care about that, either. I always knew something would happen to him. Whenever he was gone, I would wait there, waiting for what was going to happen. The other night was déjà vu. I'd seen it before. It had happened so many times in my mind already. It's terrible to say, but I am so relieved that it won't happen again." She looked at me, and her smile momentarily transformed her face. "You see, Mr. Coyne, this has liberated me."

I nodded, willing her to go on, sensing her need.

"After we got married, the magic went away. Les lost interest. I suppose I did, too, although now and then I tried to recapture it. We've been married six years. On our anniversary last fall, I prepared a special meal. Silly old broad. Candles, flowers on the table. I actually bought one of those Frederick's of Hollywood things you could practically see through. Les had promised he'd be home for supper. I was going to seduce the bastard." She smiled at me, and I wondered if she would cry again. "Of course, he didn't show up. I guess he knew all along he wasn't going to. I—"

"Omigod!" I said.

"Excuse me?"

"Gloria!"

"I don't—"

"What time is it?"

She squinted at a clock on the wall. "Quarter of one. What's the matter?"

I sighed heavily. "I had an appointment, that's all. It's okay."

"Shouldn't you call?"

"It doesn't matter," I said. "I'll call later. Finish what you were saying."

She shook her head, denying the significance of her thoughts. "I was just feeling guilty, that's all. I suppose it's a natural reaction." She picked up her napkin and dabbed at her mouth. "Thanks for listening to me."

"Don't you want to talk some more?"

"I don't want to keep you."

I reached across the table and put my hand on hers. "You aren't keeping me."

She looked down and gently withdrew her hand. "No, it's all right. I do hope that you will be able to help me with . . ."

"Sure. When you're ready, call me."

I took one of my cards from my wallet and gave it to her. She put it into her purse without looking at it. "I suppose," she said, "we ought to discuss your fee."

"That's all taken care of. Les paid me a retainer."

She smiled. "That's uncharacteristic, I can tell you that."

We walked out together into the sharp winter afternoon. I hailed a cab for Becca Katz. Then I walked back to my office. I took my time. I wasn't eager to find the message I was sure Gloria had left for me.

# 4

Julie was on tiptoes, rummaging through the top drawer of a file cabinet when I got in. I paused for a moment to admire her calf muscles. I cleared my throat. She didn't turn around.

"I'm back," I announced.

"So I see."

"Aha," I said. "I'll bet Gloria called."

Julie shoved in the drawer, turned, tilted up her chin, and strode to her desk. She picked up some papers and made a show of examining them. I went to her and leaned both hands on her desk. She turned the back of her shoulder to me.

"Am I right?" I said. "Gloria called, right?"

She flapped the papers. "I'm trying to work."

I straightened up. "Good," I said. "That's what you're paid for."

I went into my office and kicked the door shut behind me. It made a satisfyingly loud noise. I sat behind my desk and lit a cigarette, trying to savor my childish display of temper.

It didn't work. I ground out the butt and went back to the reception area. Julie was still hunched over the sheaf of papers on her desk.

"Look," I began.

She turned to face me. "My fault," she said. "It's none of my business."

"You care. I'm glad you do."

"She was awfully upset."

"I can imagine."

"I tried to cover for you. I told her you had an emergency. She said she understood perfectly, that it was fine. She might've been crying."

"I don't think so," I said. "Not Gloria."

"What are you going to do?"

"I guess I should call her."

She nodded. "Was it?"

"Huh?"

"An emergency? Where you went so fast?"

"Yes, it was. But no excuse. I should have at least asked you to call Gloria. I could have done that. I didn't think."

"That's exactly what she said. She said you weren't bad. You just didn't think sometimes."

"She slipped my mind, actually. What can I say?"

"Explain it to Gloria, not me."

"A friend of mine died. He wanted to talk to me. I got there too late."

"Oh, Brady." She reached up and touched my cheek. "Were you close?"

I shook my head. "Not that close. It was an accident. Sudden. I've been with his wife."

"Not a client, then."

"Well, yes. Lester Katz."

Julie frowned. "We don't have a client by that name."

"This was a kind of informal arrangement. I never did any work for him before. He's the private detective I've used a couple of times."

She shrugged. "I don't remember him."

"I'll be doing some work on his estate."

Julie's eyes narrowed. "This wife. Young, not bad-looking, right?"

– 28 –

I smiled wearily. "Oldish, faded. Nice lady. Not what you're implying."

She smiled brightly. "I wasn't implying a thing. Brady Coyne. Not me." The smile faded. "Is she all right? This oldish, faded wife?"

I held out my hand, palm down, and wiggled it. "About what you'd expect. Les was in a coma for about thirty-six hours. Came out of it long enough to ask for me. Then I guess he died. Hit-and-run, it was, right outside their house. She found him in the street. She seems strong, resilient. I expect she's got some tough times facing her."

"You'll help her."

I nodded. "Yes."

"Good. And now that you're back . . ."

"Sure. I'll face the music. I'll call Gloria."

I went back to my desk and punched out Gloria's phone number. It rang several times, and I was about to hang up when she answered.

"It's me," I said cheerfully.

"Oh. Hello."

"I'm sorry."

"Hey. No sweat. I really didn't expect you anyway, I guess. You said it was dumb. I should've known you couldn't handle it. Just as well, probably. You would've just felt you had to put on your evasive, distant performance for me."

"I don't do that."

She laughed.

"Actually," I said, "something came up."

"Sure. I figured it did."

"No, really. A friend of mine was in the hospital. He came out of a coma and asked for me. I had to—"

"You really don't have to tell me, Brady. It doesn't matter."

"I was planning to go to the Iruña. I was looking forward to it."

I heard her sigh. "After all these years, you don't have to do this. Don't try to protect me. I don't need it. It was a silly idea."

"It's true, though. About my friend. It's also true that I forgot about our—our date. I don't know. Maybe I wouldn't have gone anyway. Maybe you're right. Maybe I couldn't handle it."

"Don't worry about it, Brady. You'll grow up one of these years. Thanks for calling. We'll keep in touch." I thought I detected a catch in her voice. She hung up before I could say anything else.

I tried to console myself with cynical thoughts about the female gender, but, as usual, that didn't work.

A week or so later, Becca Katz called me. "You said you'd help me try to get Les's affairs in order," she said. "Does the offer still hold?"

"Of course. That's what lawyers are for." *Pro bono*, I thought. "Why don't we make an appointment. You can bring his papers in."

She hesitated. "The problem is . . ." she began. And then she stopped.

"What is it?"

"He kept his records in his office. I'm—oh, this is silly of me, I know. I went over there yesterday. I stood outside the building. I couldn't go in. You see, I never went to his office. It was his place. Like a sanctuary for him, I guess. I mean, it's not that Les and I had this great, romantic marriage. But—I am sad. I miss him. And going there felt like a violation. As if I were spying on him. Am I making any sense at all?"

"It's how you feel," I said. "We'll go together, then."

"Would you? Would you go with me?"

"Sure. That's something else lawyers are for."

I agreed to pick her up at her apartment in Somerville. She gave me directions, and I drove out there that afternoon.

Sooty snowbanks lined both sides of the street where Les Katz had lived with Becca. A blue Volkswagen had been plowed under for the winter. With cars lined along one side of the street, there was barely enough room for two to pass each other. Between the sidewalk and the street stood an untidy row of amputated old dead elms, the stumps of their branches stark against the gray winter sky. Squat, square houses huddled close to the street, separated from each other only by the width of a driveway. They were painted brown or gray, most of them. The screens on the porches were torn. Every third or fourth telephone pole had an old backboard nailed to it. The rims hung at broken angles, shreds of old net strings drooping like torn clothes on a scarecrow.

I climbed the steps to Becca Katz's house. The screen door leading into the porch hung ajar. There were two front doors, and by each were two doorbells. I pushed the one marked "Katz."

From inside came the sound of footsteps. I heard a door creak open and then thud shut. Then I heard Becca descend the stairs. She opened the door and smiled at me. She had her coat on and a purse under her arm.

"Looks like more snow," she said as we walked to my car.

"It's coming," I said. "My knee aches." I opened the door and offered my hand to help her in.

"Thank you," she said very formally.

I went around and slid in beside her. "How are you doing?"

She shrugged. "Not that good. It takes a while, I guess."

"You're looking better."

She turned and smiled at me. "Looked pretty bad the other day, huh?"

"Oh, I didn't mean—"

She laughed. "It's all right."

She told me how to find Les's office. It was near the Medford line, not far from Tufts University. I was familiar with the area.

"How long have you known Les?" she asked as I drove.

"Quite a few years. He was recommended to me. I needed some work done. He did a good job, so I used him a few other times. It was basically a business relationship."

"He did work for you, you did work for him."

"Like that. Yes."

"He wasn't always a private detective, you know."

"Most of them aren't," I said.

"Originally he was a bridge pro. Did you know that?"

"He never mentioned it."

"Take a left up there at the lights. He started in college. He was real good. Had about a million master points. He played all the tournaments on the East Coast. Rich ladies would call him, pay his expenses plus a fat fee to fly somewhere for a weekend to be their partner. Les could carry a weak partner. The ladies, they wanted those master points. And Les could win them. They were tigers, those ladies. Les used to call them LOL's. Little old ladies. I guess they were absolutely pitiless at the bridge table. Les spent more time playing bridge than he did going to classes when he was in college. Of course, he could get away with that. He was awfully smart. He spent a year at Harvard after graduation, going after a Ph.D. But he figured, who needed a degree?"

She paused, so I said, "I really didn't know Les that well."

"Funny he would ask for you when he came out of his coma."

Be careful, Coyne, I told myself. You really don't want to upset this woman. "He and I talked fairly recently. Hard to know what he might have been thinking."

I glanced at her. She was staring straight ahead at the blurry, winking lights of the late-afternoon traffic. Sparse, fine snowflakes sifted aslant through the headlights. Tiny drops of water materialized on the windshield. I turned on the wipers.

"You'd think," she said softly, "he would have asked for his wife."

"I imagine he suffered a lot of trauma," was all I could think of to say.

"I wish that explained it."

"Look, Becca—"

"Hey," she said. "It's all right. Don't worry about it."

We were silent for a few minutes. Then she said, "It's right up here."

She pointed to a low brick commercial building tucked

among some wood-frame multifamily homes, typical of Somerville's helter-skelter zoning system. I pulled up in front and stopped. There was a dry cleaner, a package store, a consignment clothing shop, and a real-estate office on the first floor. A doorway in the center of the building led up to the second-floor offices.

We got out of the car and entered into a tiny foyer. Steep stairs ascended to the second floor. They were dimly lit, and the musty odor suggested disuse.

Becca said, "Up here. I guess his office is kind of grungy. He used to say that it was what his clients expected. That's why he smoked cigars. He liked to cultivate the image."

At the top of the stairs was a short corridor. Four doors opened from it. On one of them were the handpainted words "Lester Katz, Private Investigations."

Becca fumbled in her purse and came out with a ring of keys. "I got these at the hospital. He had them in his pocket when he got hit by that car."

She tried the keys, and the third one worked. She hesitated before opening the door. "Go ahead," I said. "It's okay."

She pushed the door open. I followed her in. I felt along the wall beside the door until I found the switch. I flipped it on.

I heard Becca take a quick breath. She whispered, "Oh."

A chair was tipped over. The drawers of the file cabinets hung open. Papers were scattered across the desk and heaped randomly on the floor. The carpet was turned back.

Les's office had been ransacked.

Becca pressed herself back against me. She was staring at the obvious evidence of a burglary.

"Kinda looks like my apartment," I said brightly.

She glanced over her shoulder at me, not smiling.

I shrugged. So she didn't have much of a sense of humor. "Sorry."

We went inside. She stood in the middle of the room amid the rubble and turned slowly, studying the entire 360 degrees of it. When she had come full circle and returned her gaze to me, she was nodding her head. Her mouth was a thin, hard line. She narrowed her eyes. "I want to know what the hell is going on," she said softly.

I started to speak, but she held up her hand. "Wait, okay? Don't try to protect me. I've got a right to know."

"What are you talking about?"

"I mean, all of a sudden it's pretty clear. Lester gets run over at two in the morning. His office is broken into. He asks for you in his one minute of consciousness before he dies. Now. You tell me what's going on, and please don't lie to me this time. Because I need to know the truth. And I really can handle it. Okay?"

I nodded. "Okay."

"Les," she said. "He was murdered, wasn't he."

# 5

There was a small sofa against the wall. I took Becca's hand and led her to it. We sat down together.

"Was Les murdered?" she said. "There's no reason not to tell me."

"You're right," I said. "The answer is, I don't know. But it's possible."

"What do you think?"

I shrugged. "I guess I think he might have been, yes."

From somewhere in the room came a sudden beeping sound. Five or six quick beeps, a pause, and then another series of beeps. Then silence.

"What the hell is that?" I said.

Becca got up and went to the desk. She bent beside it, and when she straightened up she held a telephone. The receiver was off the hook. She placed it on the desk and returned the receiver to its cradle. Then she came back and sat beside me.

"We ought to call the police, don't you think?" she said.

"Let me try to get your friend Kerrigan." I went to the phone and dialed the emergency number for the Somerville police. An efficient woman's voice informed me that Officer

Kerrigan was on the night shift and wasn't available. I told her that it regarded a possible homicide. She told me to hold, and a few seconds later a man's voice told me he was Sergeant Rowe and I should talk to him.

"I'd rather talk to Kerrigan."

"Kerrigan isn't here. Who is this?"

"Look," I said, "I'm trying to be a good citizen. But it's Kerrigan I want to speak with. Can you get him for me, or shall I hang up now?"

"Mister, if you know something about a homicide—"

"Kerrigan knows what I know already, and I'm a lawyer, so don't try to tell me the law. Can you do it or not?"

I heard him expel his breath. "Why don't you give me your name and where you can be reached. I'll try to get ahold of Kerrigan for you. He's probably home having his supper."

I gave Sergeant Rowe my name and read the phone number off Les's telephone. Then I hung up.

I went back and sat beside Becca. "They're going to try to get a message to Kerrigan. He should call us here."

She was smiling at me. "You don't fool around, do you?"

"People will push you around if you let them."

She nodded. "So now we wait."

"Right."

She got up and began to move around the room, touching things. From the floor she picked up a book, glanced at it, and put in on the desk. She bent and poked randomly through the litter of papers. She wandered to the single window that looked out onto the dark Somerville street. She stood before it, her forehead resting against the sooty glass. Then she moved back to the desk. She sat in the chair behind it, rocking slowly, staring up at the ceiling. Then she swiveled around and looked at me.

"So tell me," she said.

I nodded. So I told Becca Katz about the conversation I had had with Les at Hung Moon's restaurant the previous Thursday afternoon.

"If Les did what I recommended," I said, "the husband

could easily have figured out that he was going to tell the wife what he knew.''

"And," said Becca softly, "a man might kill to prevent that from happening."

I nodded. "It's possible. Anyway, the next thing that happened was that Les asked for me from his deathbed. Seems logical that he might've wanted to tell me something about this case. At least, I can't think of anything else he might want to say to me. Assuming he was rational at the time."

The phone rang. Becca started to pick it up, but I gestured at her not to. "I'll get it," I said. "It's Kerrigan." I went to it and picked up the receiver. "Yes?" I said.

There was a perceptible hesitation. Then a woman's voice said, "Mr. Katz?" Another pause. "Is this Mr. Katz? The private investigator."

"Who is this, please?"

"I'm trying to reach Lester Katz. Do I have the right number?"

"This is Les Katz's office. He's not here right now. May I take a message?"

I heard her breathe into the telephone. Then I heard a click.

I turned to Becca. "They hung up."

"Who was it?"

"They wouldn't leave their name."

"Why do you say 'they'? It was a woman, wasn't it?"

I nodded. "Probably a client."

She smiled crookedly. "Probably a lover. It's okay. Will you please stop trying to protect me? It's very charming, this old-fashioned chivalry, or whatever you want to call it, and I appreciate it. But you're not helping me."

"Yes. I'm sorry. You're right."

"Les had lovers."

"You told me that."

She smiled. "It probably sounds like I'm obsessing on the subject. I'm not, though. I got used to it." She combed her fingers through her hair. "You think this man, then, this one who paid Les money for the photos, you think he killed him, right?''

I shrugged. "I don't have a shred of proof, but it makes some sense."

"What was the man's name? Somebody should question him."

I spread my hands, gesturing at the disarray in the office. "I don't know. Les never mentioned a name. But I bet it's the same one who who made this mess. He came to steal his file so we wouldn't be able to figure it out."

She nodded. "That would fit. So if we could learn who did this, who this man was that Les was spying on, we'd know who killed him."

"Maybe."

"Except the file that has his name on it is probably gone."

"Likely. Did Les keep his photos and tapes in the office here, too?"

She widened her eyes. "As a matter of fact, no, he didn't. He has a little office at home. He's got a lot of that stuff there." She suddenly turned down the corners of her mouth in a gesture of disgust at herself. "There, listen to me. Still talking about him in the present tense. Anyway, Les wasn't very well organized. I mean, keeping his files here, but the other stuff there."

I shook a Winston from my pack and lit it. "Good thing for us, though. It's a long shot, but Les described the kinds of photos he got of the man. If it's true what he said, that he did keep the negatives, then maybe—"

"Maybe we can get a picture of the man with his woman friend. Yes."

"A long shot," I repeated.

The phone rang again. I picked it up. "Yes?"

"Is this Mr. Coyne?"

"Yes."

"Kerrigan here. What's up?"

"I'm at Lester Katz's office with Mrs. Katz. The place has been burglarized."

He was silent for a moment. Then he said, "You think . . . ?"

"I think it could be a coincidence," I said. "On the other hand . . ."

"I get it," he said. "Kill the guy, then get your name out of his files, and you're home free."

"Possible, huh?"

"So what's missing?"

"Only one person could tell us."

"And he's dead," said Kerrigan.

"Right." I glanced at Becca. She was watching me solemnly.

I heard Kerrigan sigh. "We'll be right over. Don't touch anything."

I hung up and turned to Becca. "The police are on their way."

She nodded. "So what are we supposed to do?"

"We wait."

They arrived fifteen minutes later. Kerrigan was there, and a detective named Whiting, whose trench coat was more rumpled than Peter Falk's, and three forensic experts. Becca and I went out into the narrow hallway to let them work. After a few minutes Kerrigan came out and joined us.

"Mrs. Katz," he said, "is anything missing from your husband's office?"

She shrugged. "I have no idea. I've never been here before."

"Well, did he keep anything valuable here, do you know?"

"I don't think so. Les didn't have valuable things."

"Artwork, a coin collection, like that?"

"No. I don't know."

He looked at me. "We're following up on the hit-and-run the way we routinely would do it."

"Anything turn up?"

"Not yet."

"You'll keep me posted?"

"Sure. You, too."

Kerrigan went back into Les's office. He closed the door

behind him. Becca and I wandered down to the street. Fine snowflakes still drifted down from the dark sky. I smoked a cigarette. Becca leaned back against the brick wall, hunching her shoulders inside her coat.

The policemen paraded out of the building about an hour after they arrived. Whiting, the detective, paused beside us. "You can go back up there if you want. We're done."

"Already?" said Becca.

Whiting paused to light a cigar. "What did you expect?" he said after he got it lit.

"My husband was murdered. It would seem . . ."

Whiting glanced at me and rolled his eyes.

"Did you find anything interesting?" I said.

"About twelve million smudged fingerprints. A lot of 'em yours, probably. Listen, if you can't even tell us what was taken—"

"This is probably linked with a murder, that's all," I said.

Whiting turned away. "We're working on it," he said before he ducked into his car.

I touched Becca's shoulder. "You okay?"

She huddled deeper into her coat. "I'm fine. It just seems as if they don't care."

"They're professionals. They know what they're doing."

She looked up at me. "It looks to me as if we've got to figure out who killed Les ourselves."

"We ought to check Les's collection of negatives."

She nodded. "Okay."

"Before that, we ought to go back up to the office, see what we can find."

"What will we look for?"

"I don't know. An appointment book. A scrap of paper with a phone number on it. A page torn off a calendar. Tapes. Photos."

"But they would have stolen anything like that."

I nodded. "We look anyway."

We spent nearly two hours at it. Becca looked through all the files. I searched for hidey-holes. I pulled out all the drawers to see what might be taped onto the bottom of them. I flipped through the wall calendar, looking for notes, names, numbers, initials, something in code, anything. I rolled up the rug. I probed for loose floorboards. I took the cushions off the sofa, unzipped them, and poked around inside.

It was a simple, square room, and although my imagination was limited, I was satisfied that Les had hidden nothing there. Or if he had, someone else, whose imagination at least matched mine, had gotten there first.

I went to the swivel chair and sat in it. I lit a cigarette. Becca was kneeling on the floor. Her hair hung in her eyes.

"Enough, already," I said.

She looked up at me, blinked, thrust out her lower lip, and blew at her hair. "Okay. This is frustrating. I don't know what I'm looking for."

"Let's go see if we can find those negatives."

She was silent in the car as we drove back to her apartment. The snow had begun to stick to the roads. It coated the trees and the piles of old snow. It sparkled clean and white in the fuzzy night lights. Pedestrians hunched their shoulders as they shuffled along the sidewalks. Traffic moved slowly.

When we got inside and shucked off our coats, Becca said, "I'll bet you're starved."

"I hadn't thought about it. But now that you mention it . . ."

"How about some soup?"

"Perfect," I said. "You wouldn't happen to have a wee drop of something, would you?"

She clapped her hands together once. "I'm sorry. I should have offered. What do you like?"

"Bourbon. Ice."

She smiled. "Up there." She pointed to a top cabinet. "Can you reach for me?"

I took down a bottle of Early Times. It was almost full. "How about you?"

"There's some wine in the fridge. Les didn't drink at all. I like a glass of wine now and then."

She poured our drinks. We clicked glasses next to the sink. "To . . . ?"

"To finding those negatives," I said.

She nodded, frowned, and sipped her wine. "Okay. Come on. In here."

I followed her out of the kitchen, through a sparsely furnished living room, to a little den. There was a big leather-upholstered recliner facing a television set on a low table. A bookshelf was built into one wall. There were several volumes on bridge, I noticed—lore on Italian bidding systems, opening leads, dummy reversals, the wisdom of giants like Shencken, Goren, Gerber, Stayman. There were novels, a matched set of Gibbons with gold embossing on the leather covers, some art books, a dictionary. Jammed here and there on the shelves among the books were old newspapers and magazines and folders thick with papers.

Stacks of shoe boxes teetered precariously against one wall. A dozen, at least. And beside the shoe boxes were three large cardboard cartons.

Becca pointed to the boxes. "I think his photographs and tapes and stuff are in there. Somewhere."

It wasn't that difficult. The cardboard boxes contained tape cassettes. They were unlabeled. But Les hadn't mentioned tapes to me, so I assumed there was no purpose to listening to all of them.

The shoe boxes contained slender glassine envelopes of negatives. Thousands of them. Each shoe box was labeled with a year. One of them bore the inscription "current."

So we sat crosslegged on the floor and the two of us began to slide negatives out of their envelopes and hold them up to the light.

"It's hard to tell what I'm seeing," Becca observed.

"Look for a man and a woman. Les mentioned them getting into and out of a cab. Sitting on a park bench. Coming out of a building. He said he got nothing explicit."

She rolled her eyes at me. "He failed, then, didn't he?"

I smiled. "Yes. That's what he said."

Les Katz, I quickly learned, hadn't failed very often. I was amazed at the number of people who made love in automobiles and rowboats, or standing up against brick buildings, or under a blanket on the ground, or huddled together enveloped in a raincoat. Inventive. No wonder Les loved his work.

Lovemaking looks very different in negatives. It's an abstraction, the dark colors white and the light colors black. They looked, many of them, like the inkblots shrinks show people to diagnose schizophrenia, or like tricky optical illusions such as the one that looks either like a vase or two female profiles, and you have to make a conscious mental adjustment to see it both ways. In Les's negatives, faces and bare breasts were black, shadows white. I had to translate that reversal consciously as I examined the negatives.

Some of the strips had pictures of people doing ordinary things. These I examined carefully. But virtually all of the strips had at least one shot of something explicit.

"Hey!" said Becca. She held a strip of negatives to me.

I took it from her and held it up to the light. "This might be it," I said.

The strip showed three successive shots of two people seated on a bench. Then the same couple stepping out of a taxi. He had snapped them through a long lens, I figured, because many of them were just head and shoulder shots. It was impossible to judge the quality of the photos. But I was certain that prints would show identifiable faces.

"Here's another one," said Becca. I took it. One seemed to be a long shot taken from an unusually low angle. Several people were moving into and out of a building. A second was a closer shot of the same scene, with many faces in it. Three pictures were very blurry, as if something had moved in front of the lens. Traffic, maybe.

I stood up and slipped the negatives into the inside pocket of my jacket. Then I held both hands down to Becca. She took them and I helped her stand up. We retrieved our drinks. Both glasses were empty.

"Now what?" she said.

"Now? Now we have that soup."

"No, I mean . . ."

"After the soup, and after the brandy, if you've got any, you run yourself a hot bath and get some sleep. And I will get some prints made. Then we'll know what we have."

She took my hand and led me back to the kitchen. I refilled both of our glasses. Then I perched on a stool and watched her open a can of soup and dump it into a pot. She turned the heat on under it. "Want a salad or something?"

"Terrific," I said. "My appetite is returning."

She sipped her wine. "Those negatives. Progress, huh?"

"Don't get your hopes up. Even if we get faces that are identifiable, I'm not sure where we go from there."

She pressed her lips together. "Of course. We wouldn't have names to go with the faces. I never thought of that."

"Hey," I said. "First things first. We'll figure out something."

She came over to me and stood in front of me, wedging her hips between my knees. She put her hands on my shoulders. "Tell me something, Brady Coyne," she said softly.

"Anything."

Her eyes searched mine. "Tell me the truth."

"Sure."

"Did Les really pay you? I mean, are you really his attorney? Did he really give you a retainer? Or are you some kind of nice guy?"

I put my hands on her waist and drew her closer to me. I kissed her forehead. "Les paid me," I said quietly. "Honest. You can't get away with accusing me of being a nice guy."

She leaned away from me and smiled. "Why don't I believe you?"

"Now, Becca. If I'm going to be your lawyer . . ."

She stepped away from me. "I know, I know. Anyway, the soup's almost ready and I haven't even started that salad."

# 6

"Hey," said Charlie, doing his imitation of an old Jackie Gleason character, "what's that slop you're eating?"

"*Calamari*," I said, impaling a hunk of what looked like old inner tube on my fork and waving it at him. "Yum."

"That is squid."

"By any other name, Charlie. You ought to try this *calamari*. Nobody can prepare it like Marie."

"I always thought," he said, "that eating stuff like squid and eel and brains and thymus glands and the lining from cow bellies was nothing more than a goddamn affectation. I mean, let's face it, nobody really likes that shit."

"I do. I love sweetbreads and tripe. Also kidneys and livers and tongue."

"Bullshit. *Calamari* is just a joke. The Italians give it a different name, foist it off on non-Mediterranean types like you, and chuckle up their shirtsleeves."

I took a big bite. "Mmm. Delicious. You really ought to try the *calamari*. Where's your sense of adventure?"

Charlie poked at his manicotti. "*Chacun à son goût*," he muttered. "Pour me some more wine, huh?"

I refilled our glasses from the carafe of red that Marie always serves Charlie and me on the house. We ate in silence for a few minutes. Then Charlie looked up at me. "Okay. Let's have it, boy. You don't offer to buy me lunch unless you're after something."

"I need a sounding board," I said.

Charlie McDevitt and I had roomed together at Yale Law School. Afterward he became a prosecutor with the Boston office of the U.S. Justice Department. He was just about my best friend, the one man I trusted without reservation. We fished and played golf together, bet lunches on the outcomes of every sports event we could think of, and from time to time did each other professional favors.

The truth was, Charlie helped me a lot more than I helped him. Neither of us paid the least attention to the balance sheet.

I told Charlie how I had inherited Becca Katz as a client, and how I seemed to have blundered into a situation where I was doing a lot of work for ten dollars. As I related the chronology of events, Charlie's grin grew increasingly broad. When I paused to shove another hunk of *calamari* into my mouth, Charlie said, "You always did have that streak in you. What was it you wanted to make a career of back there in New Haven?"

"Civil liberties," I said.

He spread his hands. "Now you're doing *pro bono* work for bereaved widow ladies. You've found your niche. I never thought it was right you should be making all that money holding hands with rich old ladies anyway. So now you're doing good works. My congratulations."

"You don't think I should tell her?"

"Too late, old buddy. You want to tell her you lied to her?"

"Guess I can't," I said dolefully. "It's not that I mind helping her. Frankly, Charlie, the whole thing is complicated by the fact that, ah . . . ."

He tilted back his head and opened his mouth. "Ahh," he

said, signifying a rush of understanding. "The widow lady, huh?"

I nodded. "I'm not very proud of myself."

"You felt sorry for her."

"Something like that. I mean, things were going all right. We found those negatives, she fixed soup and made a nice salad, and afterward I was all set to leave. She said, why not have a brandy before I went. It was snowing outside, you remember, one of those soft snowstorms that makes it seem warm and cozy indoors. We'd had a couple of drinks before we ate. All that tension. She put on this record. Some guy playing a flute. Sexy music. Ah, hell, Charlie."

"So she dragged you off to bed, kicking and screaming."

"Nah. It wasn't like that. She started talking about Les again. She's sad, but she's relieved, too. She tells me how they had no sex—not like she's complaining, and not really like she's hinting at anything. Very matter-of-fact. Just a big void in her life, which she realized she had succeeded in suppressing. Charlie, she's not that attractive. Not objectively. But she's got a great sad smile, and all the funny parts of her seem to fit together pleasantly. Makes you want to hug her, you know?"

"So you did. Hug her."

I shrugged. "I meant nothing by it. It sort of evolved into something else. And now—"

"Now you don't know how to deal with her."

I found that last hunk of *calamari* amid the tangle of linguini on my plate. I maneuvered the *calamari* onto my fork and then pointed at Charlie with it. "I think she might be in love with me," I said.

"She's not in love with you, counselor," he said. "But she may think she is. Which could turn out to be a whole lot worse." He took a big gulp of wine and wiped his mouth on the back of his hand. "The lady's gotta be real vulnerable just now. Be careful, pal. You're kinda vulnerable yourself."

I nodded sourly. "I keep falling short of this image of myself."

"Hey, we all do. Reminds me of what happened to Burleigh Whitt. You ever meet him?"

I shook my head.

"Used to be in enforcement with Interior. I thought maybe he went fishing with us once. Anyway, Burl was a kid out of the Maine woods, full of piss and vinegar. He always hated the paperwork, and finally a few years ago he quit and got a job as a game warden back home in the Pine Tree State. They put him way the hell and gone up there where there aren't even any towns. Just quadrants on a topographic map. He hadn't been there long when he caught a rumor that this old-timer seemed to be bringing home fish by the sackful. Burl figured he had to be doing something illegal. Being new and unknown around there, Burl was able to wangle an invitation with the old guy to go fishing with him, and—"

"Charlie," I interrupted, "is this one of your stories?"

"I don't know what you're talking about," he said. "You ask Tiny Wheeler. He knows Burl. Anyhow, Burl meets the old fella at the crack of dawn, they take one of those back roads to this little pristine lake way back in the woods. Supposed to be full of salmon. They climb into the old guy's boat and motor to the far end. Old guy cuts the engine. 'This here's a hot spot, ayuh,' he says. Then he reaches under his seat and hauls out a big gunnysack. He shoves his hand into the sack and pulls out a stick of dynamite. He lights it and flings it overboard. It explodes in the water, and a minute later there are all these giant salmon floating belly-up in the water. The old guy gets out the oars and he rows around, sorting out the big fish and tossing them into the boat."

"Charlie—"

He held up his hand. "So they're sitting there, the rowboat practically shipping water from that load of big fish, and Burl says to the old guy, 'Okay, buddy. I got you. Dynamiting fish is illegal, and I'm your new warden.' The old guy looks at him and nods. 'Ayuh,' he says, 'I know who you are.' And he reaches into that sack and pulls out another stick of dynamite. He lights it and hands it to Burl. 'Now it's your turn to try some fishin', son,' he says."

I sighed deeply. "This really happened, huh?"

Charlie traced an X over his heart. "Swear it," he said. "There's a point to that story, Brady."

I nodded. "Yeah, I get it. Now I'm the one holding that stick of dynamite, right?"

He grinned. "Good luck, pal."

"I'm not sure you've earned your free lunch today."

He shrugged. "Think about it."

I nosed my BMW into the driveway and sat there for a few minutes. High mounds of snow rose up along the sides. I wondered if Gloria had persuaded Joey to do his chores, or if she had hired a neighborhood kid to do the shoveling.

Under its mantle of snow, the familiar Garrison colonial looked smaller than I remembered it. It was still painted gray, the way it always had been. But now the shutters were black. I had always painted them dark green. I liked the green better.

When Gloria and I bought that house nearly twenty years earlier, we assumed it would be where we would raise our two young boys to manhood. Wellesley, Massachusetts, seemed just the place for a young, upwardly mobile family to make their headquarters as they chased after the American Dream. Prosperous suburbia, thence to competitive Ivy League colleges for the boys, while Papa made lots of money out of other people's legal difficulties, and Mama had the leisure to snap artsy photographs.

We joined the country club.

We subscribed to the local theater company.

Gloria was elected president of the elementary-school PTA.

I canvassed the neighborhood on behalf of the American Cancer Society.

The boys played Little League baseball and Pop Warner football.

I coached their teams.

And Gloria and I got divorced.

The American Dream.

In the first few years after the divorce, I went back to Wellesley often. I mended broken things. I picked up the boys for weekends with their father. I allowed Gloria to persuade me to stay for a drink when I brought them back on Sunday evenings.

Gradually, without planning it or discussing it or agreeing to it, I stopped visiting the house. It became Gloria's, not mine. And that was part of the separation process for us that, as I sat there smoking a cigarette in my car parked in my old driveway and recalled our aborted luncheon date at the Iruña two weeks earlier, I realized had still not been completed.

Perhaps those things never were completed.

I patted the envelope in the inside pocket of my jacket. Les Katz's negatives. Gloria, once she got free of our marriage—which took several years after the divorce—had become a professional photographer. She did free-lance work for several national magazines. I had seen her stuff, and it was good.

She had told me that she had converted the basement into a studio. The old bathroom was enlarged to make a darkroom. She could make prints for me while I waited. I suspected I might need blowups of faces, once I got a look at what was on those negatives. She could do that for me, too.

I had called her that morning. "Gloria," I said, mustering as much cheerful formality as I could, "I need your professional expertise."

"He needs me," she said. "*Mirabile dictu*. What is it, Brady?"

"Could you make some prints for me from a set of black-and-white negatives?"

"Mail them over. It's no problem."

"I need them today, actually."

"Oh." She hesitated. "You want to bring them out, is that it?"

"I guess it's the only way."

She paused again. "You haven't been here in years. Are you sure . . . ?"

"Look, if it makes you uncomfortable . . ."

"That's not it. I just assumed . . ."

I knew better than to tell Gloria her assumptions were wrong. She always interpreted that to mean I thought she was stupid. "I really need a hand here," I said. "Mind if I bring the negatives over and wait while you do them?"

She sighed. She sounded relieved, somehow. "No, that's fine."

I got out of the car and went to the front door. She opened it. She was wearing tight blue jeans and a baggy shirt with the tails flopping. She was barefoot. She seemed to have lost a little weight in appropriate places since the last time I had seen her. I knew better than to mention it to her.

"Come in, Brady."

I went in and took off my topcoat. I started to hang it in the closet in the foyer. Then I hesitated and handed it to her.

She seemed uncertain what to do with it. She looked sideways at me and grinned. "I was going to hang it in the closet. Where your stuff goes."

"That's what I started to do."

We went into the living room. She laid my coat on the sofa. I looked around. None of the furniture looked familiar.

"Well," she said.

"Your hair," I said. "It's different."

She touched her head. "It'll look better when the perm grows out a little. I'm starting to get some grays."

"It looks good. You look good."

She rolled her eyes. "You never used to compliment me. I think I like it." She touched my cheek with her forefinger. "You look good, too, old man. You're getting little wrinkles around your eyes. Looks distinguished."

"I'm getting big wrinkles all over," I said.

"You want a drink or something?"

I shook my head. "Thanks, no. I'd really like to see what's on these negatives."

I pulled the envelope from my jacket pocket and handed it to her. She slipped the negatives from their glassine protector and held them up to the light. "These were taken through a long lens," she said, squinting. "At least a three-hundred-millimeter, I'd say. Maybe five hundred. Very shallow depth of focus. Doesn't look too sharp on most of them. Well, let's go see."

I followed her down into the basement. When I had lived there, it was what we called a rumpus room. It had been paneled with cheap imitation oak and carpeted with rubberized indoor-outdoor green stuff. The boys kept their toys down there. There had been a small television, which Gloria and I dutifully restricted to Channel 2. Both of our boys, to our confusion, had been hooked on Mr. Rogers.

Now the paneling was genuine pine. Bookcases lined one wall. Track lighting along the ceiling played selectively on several framed photographs. There was an antique rolltop desk in one corner and a big square butcher-block table. Behind a locked glass-door cabinet were shelves containing Gloria's cameras and the other tools of her trade. She had accumulated a lot of gear since I had lived there.

"This place looks great," I said.

"Different, huh? I had a designer plan it for me. She drew the specs, picked out the carpet and the furniture and everything. It's my office, all deductible. Here, peek into the darkroom."

She opened the door to where the little bathroom had been. Now it was a large rectangular room, with a double stainless steel sink, a counter of trays, shelves of chemicals, enlargers, and lots of other machinery I didn't recognize.

"Nice," I said.

"Why don't you relax out there and I'll get to work. There's a bar in the cabinet beside the desk. Help yourself."

She closed the door, leaving me alone in the rumpus room. No, Gloria's office. I looked around for an ashtray. There was none. I went to the bar. I found it well stocked, although there was no Jack Daniel's. Just like Gloria, I thought, not to have my favorite sour mash Tennessee sippin' whiskey on hand. All the booze struck me odd, at first. Gloria had never been much of a drinker. A little wine with a meal, perhaps, and an occasional gin and tonic on a summer's evening. But then I remembered that this was her place of business. She met clients here. It was hard for me to visualize Gloria meeting with clients—conferring, bargaining, selling. That wasn't the Gloria I had been divorced from eight years earlier.

I poured two fingers of Wild Turkey—not a bad bourbon, but not Jack Daniel's—into one of the expensive glasses I found stacked there. There was a built-in icemaker. I fished out a small handful of oddly shaped cubes and dropped them into my drink. Then I wandered around the room. It was, in part, a gallery.

After our divorce, Gloria began to do some portrait work. Children, mostly, the occasional wedding and bar mitzvah. She had a knack, I knew, for persuading people to look natural.

Eventually she moved into the magazine work. She specialized in photographing architecture. She did a big job on Newport a few years earlier, a lot of color work on the changes that were being wrought on the grand old buildings along the waterfront: Several of the pictures were framed and hung on the walls of my old rumpus room.

I studied Gloria's work. It looked very good to me—technically sound, but more than that, she had a gift for capturing the spirit of a building by clever use of angle and light.

I sat in one of the Scandinavian Design chairs and riffled through a photography magazine. It took me a while to identify the source of the uneasiness I was feeling.

There was no trace of me left in this house. None of my coats hung in the closets upstairs. The furniture I used to lounge on in the living room was gone. The paint I had painfully spread over the moldings and baseboards had been covered. The carpets I had trod upon had been replaced.

Now it was Gloria's place. Not mine. She had cleared me away. I guessed she had done with her mind and her heart what she had done with her house.

That insight should have relieved me. It was what we both wanted to happen when we split. But now, seeing the evidence, I felt sad.

I poured myself another drink and settled down with an

article that described how to photograph constellations. This was not something I expected ever to try.

Gloria had been in there for a little over half an hour when she opened the door to the darkroom. "Why don't you come in?" she said.

There were a dozen or so eight-by-tens laid out on a table. "Don't touch them," she said. "They're still damp."

I looked them over. "They're not that good, are they?"

She nodded. "Without a tripod you just can't get quality stuff with a long lens."

"The man who took these wasn't especially interested in quality."

Gloria shrugged. "His exposures are all okay. Probably used a programmed camera. But there's a definite tremor, and the focus is shaky. I'd guess he was using a fast film. It's pretty grainy. What are these for, anyway?"

I pointed to one of the pictures. "This man, I think. I wanted to know what he looked like."

The photograph showed a man and a woman seated close together. The woman was in quarter profile. The man was nearly full face. "Do you see this man in any of the other shots?"

We looked them over together, bending over the table, our shoulders touching. Gloria pointed to one of the pictures with the eraser end of a pencil. "Here. This is the same man."

This shot was taken from a distance. The camera seemed to be aimed upward, as if the photographer had been lying on the ground. It showed a number of people entering and leaving a building. One of those who was facing the camera did indeed appear to be our man. He wore dark-rimmed glasses. He had a long, thin face. He was bareheaded, revealing a broad forehead and light, receding hair.

"Let's find another shot of the woman," I said.

Again we pored over the pictures. The woman appeared in most of them, but there was no full-face shot. In profile she appeared to have a slightly upturned nose, dark hair cropped close at the nape of her neck and brushed back on the sides so that her ears showed. I picked out the best of them. "Can you blow up her face on this one? And this one of the guy?"

Gloria nodded. "Sure. They'll look pretty fuzzy, but I can do it. Anything else?"

She was standing close beside me. I touched her cheek with the back of my hand, and she tilted her face up to me. "That's all," I said. "I appreciate it."

She smiled quickly and turned away. "Sure. Go away."

I went back upstairs, put on my coat, and went out to the front steps to smoke a cigarette. All of that history, and yet Gloria seemed a stranger to me. An attractive stranger, I admitted. I tried to push away the quick flash of her smile, the hurt that dwelled in her eyes, the touch of her skin. She would make my pictures for me and I would thank her and leave. All the rest was reflex.

The afternoon sun had already sunk behind the row of expensive suburban homes across the street. The cloudless sky was the color of ice. A short winter day, quickly passed, like so many of the days in my life. Gone and forgotten in that great headlong rush toward the end of it.

I snapped my spent Winston toward the snow and went back inside. A chill had penetrated to my spine, and I wasn't sure that it was only the dry January air.

When Gloria emerged from her darkroom, she found me sitting at her desk looking for photos of nudes in her magazines.

She stood in the doorway, leaning her hip against the jamb. "Want to take a look?" she said.

I stood and moved toward her. She watched me, her eyebrows arched perhaps a millimeter, her lips parted as if she were about to speak. I held out my hand to her, palm up. She reached out slowly and took it, her eyes never leaving mine. Then she moved against me. She tucked her chin and put her face against my chest. "Don't," she mumbled against me.

I touched her jaw with my finger. She lifted her face to look at me. "Please, Brady."

"Shh," I said. I touched a finger to her lips.

Her eyes frowned into mine. Tiny vertical lines etched themselves between her brows.

"What do you want?" she whispered.

I gripped her shoulders and pushed her gently away from me. "I'm sorry. I'm—"

I saw her hand rise, as if in slow motion. It touched my jaw, fingertips first, then palm. Then it slid around to the back of my neck as she moved against me again, and her mouth angled up and I bent to meet it. It was the mouth of a stranger, a woman I had never kissed before, awkward, exploratory, before it slid away. Her arms went around my chest and she burrowed against me. I felt her shudder. I laced my fingers in her hair and urged her head back so I could see her. There was a little smile there, now, tiny crinkles at the corners of her eyes. Fire danced in her pupils before her lids dropped and her mouth lifted again, full of sweet, sad memory and familiar pain.

"This isn't good," I said into her hair.

"Come to bed with me." A whisper against my throat.

Becca Katz had said exactly the same thing to me two days earlier. I had complied, out of what motive I didn't want to know. I had then regretted it.

"No," I said.

"Brady—"

"Come on," I said. I took her hand and led her across the room. We sat in chairs beside each other.

"Why?" she said.

I shook my head. "It's not right."

"That is no answer. Don't you—"

"I feel it. Of course. That's the problem."

She shook her head. "I don't get it."

I smiled. "Me neither. Let's have a drink."

"I don't want a drink."

"I do." I got up and poured some Wild Turkey into my glass. I fumbled for the ice cubes, grateful for an activity that occupied me. I went back and sat beside her. "Listen," I said, "it's too easy. There's a big pit there that we could fall into. We'd hurt ourselves. Don't you see it?"

She nodded, fixing me with her eyes. "Sure. I see it. Maybe I wouldn't mind falling."

"The falling part might be okay. Hitting the bottom, that would hurt. You know it would."

"You'd catch me."

I nodded. "If I did, that would be the trap. Maybe I wouldn't, though. I could hurt myself, too."

"Ah, Brady. Maybe I just don't care."

"One of us has to."

She smiled quickly. "You're the one. You always were the one who knew where the pits were."

"Look," I said, "I'm sorry. For the ten-millionth time. It's my fault. Forget it. Please."

She touched her lips with the tips of her fingers. "It's just not that simple."

"I'm sorry," I said again.

She sat there staring across the room. I watched her face. It revealed nothing. After a minute, she turned. "Do you want to see the pictures?"

I nodded. "Yes."

I followed her back into the darkroom. She had made two eight-by-tens, one each of the man's face and the woman's half profile. They were, as she had predicted, blurry and grainy. But the faces could be recognized by anybody who knew them, I felt certain.

"This is great," I said. "Thanks."

"Who are they?"

"I don't know. It's a very long story. I'm hoping I can figure out who they are from the pictures."

"How in the world do you expect to do that?"

I shrugged. "I don't know. Maybe Charlie can help me."

She found a big manila envelope and slipped all the photos she had done into it. I tucked it under my arm and we went upstairs.

"Stay for another drink?"

"No, thanks," I said. "I had a couple already. No, I better get going."

She picked up my coat and held it for me. "What I don't

understand," she said as I slipped my arms into the sleeves, "you must know a lot of compliant women."

I thought of Becca Katz. She had been compliant. But somehow the word didn't work for her. She had been lonely, empty, desperate. "I suppose so," I said.

"And I bet you don't go through great moral debates before you go to bed with them."

"It depends."

I hunched my shoulders into the topcoat and then turned around to face Gloria. She was frowning. "It depends on what?"

"On whether I like them or not."

She turned her face so that she was peering at me out of the corners of her eyes, a sly, almost flirtatious look. "Just so I understand," she said, "do you go to bed with the ones you like, or the ones you don't like?"

I smiled. "The ones I like, of course."

She shook her head slowly. "Then," she said, "I deduce that you don't like me."

I reached for the doorknob. "No," I said. "That's not it. With you it's much more complicated."

# 7

Charlie picked up a pencil and tapped at the photographs I had spread out on his desk. "Maybe if you could give me some names I could help you," he said to me.

"If I had the names, I wouldn't need your help."

"Well, I certainly don't recognize these people."

"I didn't really expect you to." I sighed and lit a cigarette. "I just figured, you've been in prosecution for a long time. There must be some tricks."

"Legwork. Paperwork. Cooperative witnesses. Plea bargains." He waved at the smoke. "No tricks, counselor."

Charlie had a lavishly furnished office high in the Federal Building in Government Center on the back side of Beacon Hill. I gazed past his shoulder at the slate-colored winter sky. The big floor-to-ceiling window looked out toward the arches of the Mystic River Bridge. Uncle Sam had spared none of the taxpayers' funds in providing thick carpeting, chrome and teak furniture, and fancy electronic gear for his employees in the Justice Department.

Charlie lounged back in his Moroccan leather swivel chair. He tapped his teeth with his pencil. "Actually, when you think about it," he said, "it's all pretty farfetched anyway. So this guy"—he pointed with the eraser end of the pencil at the photograph of the man—"knew that Katz had found out about him and his lady friend. Katz sells him the pictures. The guy doesn't trust him to keep a secret." Charlie shrugged elaborately. "Hardly a motive for murder."

"I've heard less impressive motives."

"Oh, sure. You want to talk about wackos, that's a whole 'nother thing. For instance, guy's sitting in a movie theater. Suddenly he jumps up, turns around, yanks out his thirty-eight Police Special, and pumps five slugs into the chest of the fourteen-year-old girl sitting behind him. Know why?"

I shook my head.

"The guy tells the police. 'She was crunching popcorn in my ear.' Like that explained it perfectly. Or the broad in Queens who had the barking dog. Her neighbor calls her on the phone to complain the dog's keeping the family awake. So the broad burns down their house. Said she didn't like being harassed by those phone calls. So you're right. There are less impressive motives. With crazy people, it's unproductive to bother trying to understand motives. They've just got some weird logic twisted around inside their heads. Look, Brady. I'm not sure what you want to do even if you actually do identify this guy. You plan to have him arrested or something?"

I stubbed out my cigarette. "I don't know. That's something else I'm asking you, I guess."

He began to doodle on a legal pad. "Okay. Maybe you do a little sleuthing. Find out where whatever-his-name-is was on the night in question. Sneak a look at his automobile, see if there's a big dent on the right front fender. Or see if he's had it in the body shop recently, go talk to them. Say you turn up this lady." He touched her photograph with his pencil. "Run a trick on her. Grill her a little. See what she knows. Hell, Brady. You can grill both of them. Do the separate-room routine on them. Or try hot needles under the fingernails. Hook electrodes to the guy's balls. Slap the broad around a little."

"Come on, Charlie. I'm serious."

"Me, too," he said. Then he smiled. "Look. Frankly, I don't see how you expect to identify them anyway, so it's pretty academic."

"I went through a lot just to get these pictures."

"I hate to be the one to tell you you wasted your time." He slid the photos together into a pile and tapped the edges even. He picked up his half glasses from the desk and pushed them onto his nose. Then he flipped through the photographs again. He shrugged and put down. "Sorry, pal. I get nothing out of this."

"Isn't there anything your computer can do?"

He shook his head. "Nope." He picked up the stack of pictures again. One by one he went through them, studying them more closely, placing them side by side on his desk. When he had them all spread out again he began to shake his head. Suddenly he pushed at his glasses with his forefinger and bent closer. He picked up one of the photos and held it to his face. "Wait a minute," he said.

"What? What is it?" I stood up and moved around Charlie's desk so I was standing at his shoulder.

He was holding the photograph that showed a crowd of people entering and leaving a building. "Look at this one," he said.

I did. "That's the guy, right there," I said, touching the face with my finger.

"Yeah, I know," he said impatiently. "What else do you see?"

It was little more than a dark vertical line with a lump on top of it. "I don't know what it is," I said.

Charlie sketched something onto his yellow legal pad. the sketch resembled a lollipop. "Does it look like this?"

"Yes. Nice sketch. What do you think it is?"

"I *know* what it is. A streetlight."

I nodded. "Okay. Yes. That's what it looks like. So?"

"So?" He swiveled around to peer up at me. "So now we know that this guy was at a place that maybe you can find. Where do they have streetlights like this one?"

"Up on the Hill?"

"Those are a little different. Come on."

I smacked my fist into my palm. "Quincy Market, right?"

"Sure. Now see what you can tell about the building."

We studied it together. It was severely out of focus, but the shape of the windows and the broad details of the facade were recognizable. "Think you could find this place, counselor?" said Charlie.

"It would be a place to start."

"It'll cost you, of course."

"Fresh swordfish at the No-Name?"

"Deal."

A ten-minute cab ride took me from Charlie's office to Quincy Market. Produce trucks still congregate at Haymarket Square in the wee morning hours to peddle their fruits and vegetables, and bums sleep in abandoned doorways, and bag ladies pick over the rotting litter on the streets, just as they always did. Only now the out-of-towners don't see it. In the headlong rush toward urban renewal during the reign of Kevin White, the squalid old marketplace was shunted out back. New brick walkways and chrome and glass edifices were erected out front. Good for business, good for tourists. The New Boston. Good for Kevin White. Now the folks from Kansas City can purchase pizza wedges topped with tofu and bean sprouts, stuffed teddy bears and plastic lobsters made in Taiwan, framed prints of the Paul Revere statue, and other remembrances of quaint old colonial Boston. And they miss the real thing just around the corner.

Quincy Market is a great place to hang around if you want to pick up lonely secretaries or bank clerks after work. There are a few good restaurants and barrooms. The best of both are still at Durgin Park, which had been there about a hundred years before redevelopment arrived.

I wandered aimlessly around the broad brick plaza, trying to match up the scene in the photograph. Although it was only midafternoon, the thick wet clouds overhead cast a dark pall over the city and made it seem like dusk.

I made a complete circuit of the marketplace. I cocked my head at the buildings, seeking angles that would include one of the lollipop streetlamps along the left edge of my view.

It wasn't working.

Although I moved briskly, the damp chill penetrated my topcoat. My ears burned, and my nose began to dribble.

I ducked into the bar at Durgin Park and climbed onto a stool. The bartender was down at the other end talking with a woman whose corn-colored hair was cut like the Dutch boy on the paint cans. She wore a pink blouse with several strands of gold around her neck. Her black skirt was slit most of the way up the side, revealing a lot of sleek thigh.

She was, I guessed, either a hooker or an attorney.

The bartender wore a black beard, so densely grown and closely trimmed that it looked painted on. "Help you, mate?" he said, moving down the bar toward me. Australian, I judged. He made a ceremonial pass with his rag at the spotless counter in front of me.

"Jack Daniel's, on the rocks."

I shucked off my topcoat and folded it on my lap. I lit a cigarette and took the sheaf of photographs out of their envelope. I studied the one with the gas lamp and the building in the background again. One more wild-goose chase in a career full of them.

The bartender set my drink and a small bowl of dry-roasted peanuts in front of me. He glanced at the photograph before he went back to the lady.

I munched peanuts, sipped my drink, smoked, and stared unfocused at the picture. My thoughts strayed to Becca Katz, thence to Gloria. I had bedded Becca without hesitation. I had refused to do the same with Gloria. I couldn't shake the feeling that I had treated them both shabbily. I found it all very confusing.

"Whatcha got there, Captain?"

I looked up. The bartender was craning his neck, trying to examine the photograph that showed the streetlamp. I turned it around for him. "I'm trying to figure out where the photographer was standing when he snapped this," I said.

I expected him to ask why, and my mind swirled with the senseless lies I could tell him.

Instead, he said, "Why, over the kiosk, mate."

"What kiosk?"

He touched the picture with his forefinger. "This is the kiosk. Bostix. Where they sell discount theater tickets, you know. Next to Faneuil Hall, Captain. I'd say the cameraman was just behind it."

It was a very blurred shape in the foreground on the right edge of the photo, a slope of low roof, a smudge of wall, little more, so shapeless that neither Charlie nor I had registered it. The streetlight on the left of the picture, as fuzzed as it was, appeared sharply focused by comparison.

"Thank you, thank you," I said. I dropped a ten-dollar bill onto the bar, stood up, and humped into my topcoat.

"Wait for your change, mate," said the barman as I turned to leave.

"Keep it. You've earned it." It could have been the same ten-spot Les had given me a couple of weeks earlier. Easy come, easy go.

Outside, hard grains of sleet fell like shrapnel from the prematurely darkened sky. Traffic moved slowly, showing fog lights. I found the kiosk positioned more or less in the middle of the plaza. I stationed myself so that it loomed on my right. The perspective was wrong, even accounting for the foreshortening effect of the long lens Les Katz had used. I crossed the street and tried again. The angle was okay. But now the streetlight was out of position, and Faneuil Hall in the background looked wrong. I crossed the street again. Slowly I walked around the kiosk. Then it dawned on me. Les had stood with his back to Faneuil Hall, shooting beyond the kiosk and up a flight of steps at the office building across the way.

I took out the photo and studied it. It fit. The building was modern, with a flat concrete exterior composed of several angled facets. The windows were square and starkly plain.

I guessed my mystery man had emerged from the building and begun to descend the steps when Les, leaning back against the wall of Faneuil Hall and looking like any other tourist, snapped the picture. It would account for the odd angle, and the way the pedestrians seemed to be superimposed against the third story of the building.

I tucked the photo back into the manila envelope and re-crossed the street. A bank occupied the street level of the building. Through the window I could see the plush cranberry carpeting and the open layout, with tiny cubicles created by a maze of shoulder-high partitions. All of the bank employees were dressed very slick. None of them seemed especially busy.

I hadn't figured out my next move. I went into the lobby. It was wide and glittery. Elaborately framed landscape paintings decorated the walls. There were two banks of elevators. At the far end crouched a family of soft chairs and an enormous sofa, all upholstered in identical rich blue material.

Next to the elevator a glass-covered black velvet panel listed all of the businesses located in the building. Twenty-two stories, six offices per floor.

I wandered over to the sofa and sat down. Now what? I could visit each of the 132 offices, show the photograph of the man who might have run over Les Katz, and see who'd be willing to identify him. On what pretext? Should I announce that this man might be a murderer? Gauche at best. Perhaps I could pass myself off as an emissary of John Beresford Tipton, bearing in my hand a check for one million dollars that was intended to screw up the life of the lucky man in the photo.

Anyway, assuming my man had actually come out of this building—an assumption that itself was a long shot—what had he been doing in it? Probably nothing memorable. A business call? Was he some kind of salesman? Or somebody's client?

Maybe he just ducked in to take a leak.

Perhaps I should go back and have another drink with the Australian barman and see if the lady with the Dutch boy haircut might like to go upstairs with me for a slab of Durgin Park roast beef.

A janitor wearing a starched gray shirt and matching pants puttered nearby. He was pushing a big canvas basket on wheels. He bent close to me and emptied an ashtray into his basket. He was whistling softly.

"Pachelbel," I said.

He turned. "Huh? You talkin' to me?"

"The canon by Pachelbel. It's what you were whistling."

"Just something I heard on the radio," he muttered. "Only station I could get that wasn't playin' that awful stuff."

"Can I talk to you for a minute?"

He was a thin, wiry man. Close to seventy, I guessed. An uneven stubble of white whiskers sprouted from his jaw. "Me?" he said. "You wanna talk to me?"

"Yes, sir. If you can spare one minute."

"Nope."

He turned away and resumed whistling. "Wait a minute. Please. Sir."

"Me still?" He had caved-in cheeks. His mouth was a thin, sour line.

"I just want you to look at a picture."

He cocked his head. "Whatever you're sellin', I ain't buyin'. Son of a bitch in the bank says his goddamn clocks are out of sync. I gotta go set 'em. Already I'm behind, having all these conversations."

I held up the photograph of the man's face to him. "Do you recognize this man?"

"Ain't got time for games," he mumbled. He started to push his basket away.

I fumbled for my wallet and withdrew a twenty-dollar bill. "Do you recognize *this* man, then?" I said, holding it in front of the photo.

He glanced over his shoulder. His eyes narrowed. "That's Andy Jackson. Old Hickory hisself."

I held out the bill to him. "Please look at my photograph."

He made Old Hickory hisself disappear. Then he squinted at the photo. "Yeah," he said slowly, "I maybe seen this guy."

"Can you tell me his name?"

He shrugged. "It ain't comin' to me very good."

I sighed and fished out another twenty. His eyes watched my hands. "Please try to remember."

He scratched his head. "It's comin'. Kinda blurry, but I'm gettin' it."

I handed the bill to him. It joined its predecessor. "Mr. Hayden," he said promptly. "Mr. Derek Hayden. Seventh floor. American Investments. Knocks his pipe out on the floor. Burns holes in the rug. Otherwise a nice fella."

He gave his basket on wheels a shove and ambled away, whistling something from *Oklahoma!* A well-rounded man, musically.

# 8

I felt pretty smug.

The feeling didn't last.

The fact was, I hadn't actually expected to learn the name of the man in the photo, so I had not planned my next move. But here it was, four-thirty on a Friday afternoon, and here I was, just downstairs from this Derek Hayden's office.

Derek Hayden. Once I was able to attach a name to the face in the photo, I composed his biography with quick, broad brushstrokes in my head. It was a harmless and sometimes satisfying hobby of mine to fashion life stories on the thinnest of evidence, such as a name and a picture and the little snippets I got from Les Katz. What was instructive was comparing my imaginings with the reality after I learned it.

It was amazing how rarely I even came close. A humbling lesson in my own proclivity to stereotype.

But I kept doing it.

Derek Hayden's father, I guessed, was a Wall Street attorney. Specialty in mergers and bankruptcies. Expert on Chapter Eleven. Raised his family on a safe, maple-lined cul-de-sac in Scarsdale, from where he commuted every day. He also rented a pied à terre in the city, where he managed to rendezvous occasionally with a certain secretary from his firm. His wife, Derek's mother, suspected but preferred not to know, inasmuch as she was well contented with the status quo, especially since it included membership at The Club with the attendant opportunities to study the moves of the young tennis pro.

Father Hayden sent his silver-spoon-fed only son to Andover, where the lad captained the crew and served as dorm monitor. On to Williams (early admission), a narrow choice over Princeton (wait-listed), where he earned leisurely B-minuses, majoring dutifully in economics, charmed the faculty wives, and interviewed so well that Harvard Business School accepted him in spite of his barely competitive academic record.

The Mount Holyoke gal to whom he was betrothed waited bravely for him to finish graduate school. They agreed that it would be sensible for her to find a nice job, live at home, and, of course, remain faithful because Derek would be studying so terribly hard. They met one weekend a month (a weekend that coincided conveniently with the young lady's menstrual cycle, although she was, of course, fitted for a diaphragm), usually in Cambridge, where Derek would rent a room for Kimberly (for that is what I named the future Mrs. Hayden) and they would screw each other into exhaustion from Friday evening until Sunday afternoon, when Derek put Kim tearfully back on the bus.

From the B. School it was inevitable that Derek, with his rugged good looks, his skill at racquet games and golf, and his presentable young bride, should rise quickly.

All the way to the seventh floor over my head.

I stubbed out the cigarette that had burned down to the filter while I was composing Derek Hayden's life story. The part about how he ran over Lester Katz one winter night seemed as if it would fit right in. And now that I knew him, I figured it was time to meet him.

I went to the elevator and jabbed the button for the seventh floor. A moment later I was deposited into a broad corridor swathed in the same cranberry carpeting I had seen in the bank on the ground floor. Somebody had a special on the stuff, or had a brother-in-law in the business.

I stood at the hub of a sort of hexagon, each side an office space with the elevator shaft at the center. I walked halfway around the core and found what I was looking for—a door with "American Investments, Inc." painted on it. Under that legend were printed the names of Arthur B. Concannon and Derek R. Hayden.

I lacked a plan. I compensated with confidence. I was pretty good at what we attorneys—and, I suppose, people in most other occupations—call "winging it." My best summations were always ad lib efforts in which I responded to subliminal cues from the judge or the jury or my learned adversary. I was always a little more keyed up when I felt less than fully prepared. The adrenaline surged more powerfully. I got psyched. It was a matter of trusting the subconscious to do its thing, to let the training and experience assert themselves.

Sometimes, to be sure, it bombed. But not usually.

So I pushed open the door and entered the hush of the office. I stood staring at the woman I had pictured when I imagined the blushing Kimberly being greeted at the bus stop by young Derek. It was, actually, uncanny, from the studiously casual styling of her short blond hair to her vanilla complexion to her tennis-trim figure that her conservative printed cotton blouse revealed but did not exploit.

She appeared to be in her midtwenties. Her name, I cleverly deduced by reading the little plaque on her desk, was Ms. Walther. And she was smiling at me.

"May I help you, sir?" Her voice contained a hint of challenge, an awareness that she was female and I was male and that there was a difference. It was not the way the imaginary Kimberly would have spoken. This one was sexier. Perhaps a shade less wholesome, and correspondingly more interesting.

"I was hoping to catch Derek before he left. He's still in, I hope."

"Mr. Hayden, you mean?"

"Right. Sure. Derek Hayden. You got a lot of Dereks who work here?"

She shifted her smile from friendly to polite. "Nope. Just Mr. Hayden."

"Well, then"—I pretended to squint at her nameplate for the first time—"Ms. Walther, it is, huh? Does your family manufacture firearms? James Bond, a dear old friend of mine, carries a Walther PPK, you know."

"Don't be silly, Mr. . . ."

"Pardon me. Coyne. Brady Coyne. At your service." I extracted one of my business cards from my wallet and with a small bow handed it to Ms. Walther. She accepted it as if it were something breakable. She read everything on it, which wasn't much. My name, business address, telephone number. She ran her forefinger over the embossed lettering. The whole process seemed to take her a long time. I sensed she was sizing me up.

Finally she looked at me. "Well, Mr. Coyne, I'm not sure that Mr. Hayden can see you just now. He's quite busy. But perhaps if you could tell me . . ."

I nodded and gave her an aw, shucks grin. "Sure. Understand. But, see, this is personal, miss. Not business. I'd truly appreciate if you could just poke your head in and tell him I'm here and that I really think he'd like to have a chat with me. Tell him I am Lester Katz's lawyer." I hesitated and made my face serious. "Lester Katz," I repeated. "That's K-a-t-z. Okay?"

"I can spell quite well, actually, Mr. Coyne. One of the things I do around here is spell words for the rich guys who never learned how. But what I'm trying to tell you is that I don't think Mr. Hayden will see you regardless of why you're here or who this Lester Katz is." She cocked her head and smiled prettily. "But I will make sure he sees your card. I'll ask him to call you. How would that be?"

I placed my hands on the front edge of her desk and bent to her. "Tell him," I said, my voice conspiratorial, "that I want to discuss the photographs he recently purchased from Les Katz. Okay? Just tell him that.''

She frowned and gazed past my shoulder. Then she looked thoughtfully at me. She reached for the telephone console on her desk, hesitated, and let her hand drop. ''No,'' she said. ''I'm not supposed to. Not if you don't have an appointment. They are very specific about this.''

I smiled broadly. ''I think Derek'd appreciate it if you used some independent judgment on this one.''

She stared at me for an instant, then nodded. ''Excuse me, sir.'' She rose from her desk and disappeared around a corner behind her, where it looked as if there was a suite of offices.

I took the opportunity to look around the reception area. I wondered what sort of enterprise American Investments really was. It sounded like one of those things private investigators like to print on their phony business cards. An impressive-sounding cover to get past certain doors and persuade folks to confide in them.

In an alcove to the right of the door grew a potted plant in a tub. It had leaves the size of a newspaper page. A fern swung from a hook in the ceiling. There were two easy chairs and a love seat upholstered in what Charlie McDevitt calls ''genuine Naugahyde, from domestically reared naugas.'' A glass-topped table bore the current issues of *Fortune*, *Business Week*, and *Time*. There were several framed prints of Audubon birds on the beige-painted walls. Otherwise the place was as antiseptic as an operating room.

I sat on one of the chairs and lit a Winston. I was disappointed they didn't stock *New Yorker* magazines. I had thought every office in America subscribed to *The New Yorker*. Julie always insisted that we had to. I don't recall ever seeing a *New Yorker* except in a waiting room.

Ms. Walther returned before I finished my cigarette. She was taller than I had judged when she was sitting. My favorable judgment on her figure, however, appeared to have been accurate.

She resumed her seat. I stood up and went to her desk.

"Well? Can I go in now?"

She shrugged. "He's not in, Mr. Coyne."

"You mean he won't see me."

She leaned forward and peered up at me. I noticed that her eyes were dark bluish-green, a most unusual color for eyes, the color of Bermuda grass, which is used on some of our better golf courses. "I mean," she said, spacing out her words for emphasis, "Mr. Hayden is not in. Which is what I said."

I shrugged. "You could have said that right at the beginning. You can appreciate my confusion."

She sighed and didn't answer. She shifted some papers on her desk.

"I mean," I persisted, "If you have to go check with somebody to ask them if they're in, a less trusting person might actually assume you're checking with the person who's not in. Except, of course, then he's in. So I figured you went in to old Derek's office. 'There's this guy, name of Coyne, says something about photographs, mentions somebody named Lester Katz, and you wanna see him, or what?' And old Derek says, 'Tell him I'm out, Beth, honey. Guy's probably selling brooms or something.' And you say, 'Well, he gave me his card, and it says on it that he's a lawyer.' And old Derek would laugh and maybe pinch your cheek or something, and he'd say, 'Well, that's probably how he fools receptionists so he can get in to sell his brooms.' And you might say, 'Well, Derek, kid, this guy looks more like a lawyer than a broom salesman,' and Derek says, 'well, Bethie, who the hell wants to talk to a lawyer this time on a Friday afternoon, huh? I mean, TGIF, right, sweets? So you wanna get rid of this guy for me? Tell him I'll call him sometime.' "

She was smiling. "Melanie," she said.

"Pardon?"

"My name is not Beth. It's Melanie. And Mr. Hayden is really and truly not in. And when he is in, he does not pinch my cheek. Or anything else. And he doesn't call me sweets, or honey, either." Her head was lowered, but I could see

– 73 –

that she was grinning broadly. She looked up, still smiling. "Honest."

"Melanie," I said. "Nice name. And if he's really and truly not in, then maybe at least you could—"

At this instant a man appeared behind her from the office suite. He had thick white hair, an unusually wide, sensual mouth, and narrow eyes that drooped on the outside corners. He was short and broad and gave the instant impression of power and confidence. He was glowering at me.

"Who is this man, Ms. Walther?"

"This is Mr. Coyne, sir. Who I mentioned to you."

"Well? What do you want?" he said to me.

"For one thing, I'd like to know why your receptionist is so much more pleasant than you are."

His frown lasted just a moment longer. Then he converted it into a professionally amiable smile. "Of course. I apologize. The end of a long week. Please excuse my manners. My name is Arthur Concannon."

He came around from behind Melanie Walther's desk with his hand extended. I took it. His grip was just firm enough, well practiced. He fixed me with his eyes when we shook, which was the same way I had learned to do it.

"May I get you some coffee, Mr. Coyne? Or a drink, perhaps?"

I shook my head. "Thanks, no. I really just wanted to talk with Derek Hayden for a minute. If he's really not here—"

"He's been out of town for a few days."

"When do you expect him back?"

"I'm not sure. You see, Mr. Coyne, Derek and I are partners. We consult frequently, but each of us has his own accounts, and for the most part we work quite independently. We do not keep tabs on each other. Except, of course, where it counts."

He smiled and I nodded. "The old bottom line," I said.

"Anyway, I really couldn't tell you when he'll be back. I suppose you'll just have to try again."

"Perhaps you could give me his home phone number. I

seem to have misplaced it. Can't even remember where he lives.''

Concannon shook his head. "I'm sorry, Mr. Coyne. It is a general principle of mine not to give out any such information. Nothing personal. I'm sure you understand.''

I shrugged. "It's up to you." I turned to Melanie Walther. "You have my card. When Mr. Hayden comes in, would you be good enough to give it to him and ask him to call me?''

She nodded. "Certainly.''

"Thanks," I said. I turned to Concannon. "Thank you, too.''

He held out his hand again, and we practiced staring at each other some more. "Sorry we couldn't help you. I'm sure Derek will be sorry to have missed you.''

I smiled. "I'm sure. But I'll catch up with him.''

As I left the office, I noticed that Melanie Walther was staring quizzically at me. It occurred to me that she might have told me more had not Concannon interrupted.

I rode the elevator back to the lobby. It was nearly five o'clock. Quitting time. On a hunch, I resumed my unobtrusive place on the sofa and watched the elevators. They were busy, spewing folks out into the lobby and then rising back up into the bowels of the building for another load.

I waited ten or fifteen minutes before Melanie Walther stepped off the elevator. I stood up. Arthur Concannon was not with her. I caught up with her before she left the building and managed to get into position to hold the door for her. It didn't seem to surprise her.

She gave me that same quizzical smile. "I wondered if you'd be here," she said, brushing past me. She paused outdoors to turn up the fake fur collar on her coat. "Whew! Nippy, huh?''

"What did you mean?''

"About what?''

"Wondering if I'd be here.''

She smiled. "If you'd try to pick me up, I guess.''

"Oh, no, Miz Walther. I'm not trying to pick you up. I just hoped you might—''

"Tell you more about Mr. Hayden. Why Arthur and I were so mysterious about it. Right. And maybe buy me a couple drinks while you're at it, huh?"

I spread my hands. "Exactly. What do you say?"

"I really don't think I should."

"Have the drink, or tell me about Derek Hayden?"

We were walking down the short flight of stairs where Hayden had been photographed by Les Katz. She moved cautiously in her high-heeled shoes on the icy steps, so I touched her elbow to steady her. At the bottom of the steps she stopped to face me. "Both, I guess. I don't think Arthur wants me to talk to you. And I don't normally allow myself to be picked up."

"I don't want to be dramatic or anything," I said, "but this may literally be a matter of life and death. I must get in touch with Hayden. It is really important."

She stared at me, her eyes rounded, as if she hoped to discover my true intent. Then she tossed her head. "Okay. You got me. If you're hitting on me, you're doing a good job of it. You got me interested. Buy me a drink."

We strolled briskly across the brick plaza past Faneuil Hall and around the greenhouses to Durgin Park. The bar was more crowded than it had been an hour earlier, but we found two empty stools and hoisted ourselves onto them. The hooker/attorney with the Dutch boy haircut had left, but the Aussie barman was still there. He came over, made a pass in front of us with his rag, winked broadly at me, and said, "Found what you were looking for, eh, mate?"

I turned to Melanie and spread my hands. "He doesn't know what he's talking about. Honest."

"Sure," she said. But she was grinning.

"What would you like to drink?"

"Vodka martini, please."

"Stirred, not shaken, like my pal James Bond, right?" To the barman I said, "Bourbon old-fashioned for me, on the rocks."

He turned to get our drinks. I helped Melanie slip her coat off. I lit a cigarette and offered her one. She shook her head

- 76 -

and rummaged in her purse for her own. I held my lighter for her. She touched my hand as she guided the flame to her cigarette.

She exhaled a long plume of smoke, then swiveled on the stool to face me. "Okay, now, Mr. Attorney, sir. What is this life-and-death stuff, anyhow?"

I reached into my jacket pocket and pulled out the envelope of photographs. I found the picture of Derek Hayden and put it onto the bar. "Is this Derek Hayden?"

She only glanced at the photo. "Sure. I thought you knew him."

"Well, actually I don't. We have a mutual acquaintance."

"Who's your client, right?"

"Yes."

"So whose life is it that's in jeopardy here? Derek's?"

I shook my head. "I'd rather not get into that. You'll just have to trust me that it's important."

"Why should I?"

"Because I have an honest face, of course."

She studied my face. Then she smiled. "Okay. I'm a sucker for tall, skinny men with gray eyes and lumpy noses. Makes me believe you got beat up trying to defend your sister's honor sometime. What do you want from me?"

"When do you expect Hayden back in the office?"

She made a show of stubbing out her cigarette. Without looking at me, she mumbled, "Mr. Concannon—"

"What about him?"

She sighed and looked up at me. "American Investments does a lot of high-risk things. It's very important for the company that our plans remain secret. Timing, getting the jump on the competitors, information—what I'm saying is that neither Mr. Concannon nor Mr. Hayden would appreciate me talking with you. Hell," she said, smiling, "they wouldn't like it if they knew I was here, even. You know?"

I nodded. "All I want to know is when Hayden is expected back. I don't care where he went, or why he went there."

"I'm trying to tell you. We don't know where he went. He just didn't show up when we expected him. Nobody knows where he is. And I know I shouldn't have told you that.''

"So Concannon didn't tell me the truth."

She shrugged. "What did you expect?"

"Okay. Fair enough, I guess." I paused as the Aussie delivered our drinks. I lifted my glass and gestured toward Melanie Walther with it. "Your health," I said.

She nodded and we sipped. I lit another cigarette. Then I said, "When did Hayden disappear?"

" I didn't say he disappeared," she said quickly. "I just said he didn't show up at the office."

"But he didn't call in sick or anything?"

"No."

"Well, then, when was it that he failed to appear?"

She frowned. "It was a week ago Wednesday. I remember, because I had to cancel an appointment, and Arthur—Mr. Concannon—couldn't fill in because it was Derek's deal, and the client was very upset. I called Mrs. Hayden. She seemed surprised he wasn't in."

A week ago Wednesday, I quickly calculated, was the day after Les Katz had been struck down by a hit-and-run automobile. Not, I decided, a coincidence. It seemed clear to me that Hayden had run over Les and then fled, probably with his mysterious ladylove, for parts thus far unknown.

"Have you talked with Hayden's wife since then?"

She nodded. "Several times, as a matter of fact. She won't say much. But I don't think she knows where he is. Arthur is extremely upset. Their system makes it very hard for them to pick up for each other. A number of things have gone sour because Derek isn't around."

"I'd like to talk to Mrs. Hayden."

"You think something has happened to Derek, don't you."

I shrugged. "I don't know."

"He lives in Harvard. They have a big old farmhouse with a view of Mount Wachusett. They keep horses for their girls."

"His number is in the phone book, then."

"I imagine so. Never looked."

I reached back into my envelope of photographs and found the one of Hayden's lover. I put it on the bar. "Do you recognize her?"

She picked it up and squinted at it. "No," she said slowly. "I'm sure I don't know her. I'm pretty good on faces. I don't believe I've ever laid eyes on this person." She put the picture down and looked at me. "What's her connection?"

I shook my head. "I'd have to speculate."

Melanie tilted her glass and finished her drink. Then she picked up her napkin and touched her mouth with it. "I really have to go."

She hesitated. My move? Simple enough. Have you made plans for dinner? Have you seen the show at the Shubert? Interested in the nighttime view of the ocean from the sixth floor of my apartment building? Are you lonely like me? Wanna fool around?

Becca Katz. Gloria.

I smiled. "Here. Let me help you with your coat."

She cocked her head, then smiled and nodded. "Thank you." She shrugged on her coat and held her hand to me. "Thanks for the drink."

"I appreciate your help, Melanie."

I watched her leave, then swiveled back to face the bar. The barman came over. He arched his eyebrows. "Have another, mate?"

"Might as well," I said.

# 9

Harvard, Massachusetts, got its name from the same John Harvard who founded the university whose law school declined me admission twenty years ago on the reasonable ground that a lanky tight end with a trick knee and mediocre grades would be unlikely to become an attorney worthy of its hallowed name, for which I was grateful, even at the time, realizing that Yale Law, which had happily accepted me, was better suited to my relatively laid-back temperament, but that, had the Crimson bestowed its blessing upon my application, it would have been a bitch to turn down.

Harvard—the village—snuggles among rolling hills and meadows a good thirty miles west of Boston, beyond Interstate 495, on the fringe of the surprisingly rural central part of the commonwealth. It has only recently been discovered by young lieutenants of high-tech, psychiatrists, architects, podiatrists, and, yes, attorneys. The solid old farmhouses, Capes, and colonials have been renovated to make them look even older than they are. Rigorous zoning laws and building codes have, so far, preserved the country flavor of the town, so that as I exited off Route 2 on Saturday morning I felt as if I had abruptly arrived in Vermont's Northeast Kingdom. The road wound through woodland, marsh, pasture, and orchard. Sheep grazed behind a recently whitewashed fence. A little farther on, the stubble of a cornfield poked up through the windswept remains of the winter's snowfall.

I descended a hill and came upon the village green—now white—rimmed with leafless old maples and beeches. Tucked between an imposing brick house and a square old country store was a real-estate office of relatively recent vintage. I parked in front and went in.

The single large room was furnished with half a dozen desks. Only one of them was occupied, that by a chubby young woman with an Orphan Annie hairdo. She was talking softly into a telephone, and when I entered she smiled and nodded to me and gestured with her free hand at a chair beside her desk. I returned her nod but chose instead of sitting to study the display of available real estate, Polaroid photos, and index cards tacked onto a large bulletin board on the wall.

Property values, I learned, were as grotesquely inflated in rural Harvard as in the more easterly parts of the state.

I heard the woman hang up. "Hi," she said. "Can I help you?"

I went over and sat in the chair beside her desk. "I'm not looking for a house."

"That's okay."

"I just want directions."

She shrugged. "Actually, I don't know the town that well. I don't live here, myself. Can't afford it. But I've got maps and stuff."

"Farm Pond Road?"

"Let's look it up." She rummaged in the bottom drawer of her desk and came up with a tabloid-size soft-covered book. She flipped it open, squinted at it for a moment, and then said, "Here we are." She turned the map so I could look at it. "We're right here," she said, touching a place on the map with her forefinger. "You go down that road out front, heading north—go left, see—and take the—one, two, three—third right. Okay? Farm Pond Road will be your second left.'' She looked up at me. I noticed that a pencil had been jammed into her hair. Only the eraser end showed. ''I remember now,'' she said. ''It's nice out there. We had a listing on Farm Pond Road last year. Didn't last long. I thought it sounded familiar.''

''I studied the map for a minute. ''Okay. I got it. Thanks a lot.''

''Glad to help.''

I went outside and climbed back into my BMW. I had gone to the public library earlier in the morning to find a phone book with Harvard listings. Derek was one of the three Haydens living in the town. I copied down his number and street address and then decided to medicate a mild case of midwinter cabin fever by driving out there rather than phoning.

Farm Pond Road turned out to be several miles into the countryside, much father from the real-estate office than it appeared on the map. I drove slowly, unsure of what I was looking for, since the phone book had not given a number to go with the street address. Melanie Walther had mentioned a farmhouse, a view of a mountain, horses. I hoped I'd be able to pick out Hayden's place.

It was easier than that. His mailbox was labeled ''Hayden'' in glow-in-the-dark stick-on letters.

I pulled into the curving driveway beside a white-shingled old farmhouse. Behind it was a small barn. A Volvo station wagon was parked in front of the barn.

I sat in my car for a minute, regretting my decision to dress in my customary Saturday morning garb—baggy old brown corduroy pants, scarred cowboy boots, turtleneck, and parka. My gray wool three-piece suit and tweed topcoat would have enabled me to present myself more credibly.

I got out and went to the door. I rang the bell, waited, peered inside into the richly carpeted foyer and beyond to a winding staircase, and listened for footsteps. I rang the bell again and waited some more before concluding that no one was inside.

I went around back. It was one of those crystal-clear winter days when the sun's light is intensified by its reflection off the snow, the air so crisp and cold that a deep breath burns the lungs. When I stepped into the dark mustiness of the barn, I was momentarily blinded, so that I heard the voice before I could see its source.

"Who's there?" she said. "Who're you, anyhow?"

"Mrs. Hayden?"

As my eyes adjusted I detected first her shape and gradually her features. She was leaning on a long-handled shovel. Beside her was a wheelbarrow. Her brown hair was cut very short on the sides and the back. She wore a red beret, blue jeans tucked into calf-high boots, several layers of sweaters, and leather work gloves.

She was tall and lanky and awkward-looking. Large eyes widely spaced, crooked nose, expressive mouth.

She was frowning at me. "I'm Brenda Hayden, yes."

"My name is Coyne," I said. I took a step toward her and then, as I noticed her grip tighten on her shovel, I stopped. "I'm a lawyer. An associate of Lester Katz."

She came toward me, her head cocked to one side in inquiry. "Who?"

"Brady Coyne," I said. I took out my wallet and removed a business card. I held it toward her as if it were a peace offering.

"No, I mean the other name."

"Oh. Lester Katz. You know Les Katz."

She stood in front of me and absentmindedly took the card from me. She didn't look at it. "I don't know anybody named Les Katz."

I tried to remember Les's description of Hayden's wife. He'd told me she had spectacular blond hair and an equally spectacular body. He'd likened her to Farrah Fawcett. This Brenda Hayden was the antithesis of Farrah Fawcett.

I was confused. "I'm looking for Derek Hayden's wife. Maybe—"

"I'm Derek Hayden's wife. Do you know something . . . ?"

She stopped and looked down at my card. Then she looked up again. Her eyes were dark. In the dimly lit barn they seemed to be all black pupils. I read sadness and confusion in them.

"The Derek Hayden who works for American Investments?" I said.

She smiled and nodded. "Oh, so you're here on business, then. Well, Derek isn't here now."

I shook my head. "I'm not here on that kind of business. I'm looking for your husband. I was at his office yesterday. They said they haven't seen him for over a week. So I thought . . ."

I let my voice trail away to the implied question. Brenda Hayden studied me for a minute. Then she said, "Come on inside. We'll have coffee. We can talk."

I followed her into the big kitchen in the back of the farmhouse. It was dominated by a big maple hutch, which displayed a collection of antique pewter. A cold woodstove hunkered in the corner. I sat at the oval table and she poured two mugs of coffee. Then she sat down across from me.

"You're an attorney," she said. "What do you want with Derek? Is he in some kind of trouble?"

I shrugged. "Maybe. I'm not sure. I need to talk to him, that's all. I was hoping he'd be here. Can you tell me how to reach him?"

"What does this have to do with what's-his-name—Les Katz?"

"Just that you hired Les to follow your husband, and Les was my friend."

She frowned. "And why did I hire Les Katz to follow my husband?"

"You thought he was having an affair, evidently."

She peered at me over the rim of her coffee mug. She seemed faintly amused. "That," she said after a long moment, "is a crock."

"A crock?"

"I hired *nobody* to follow Derek. I do *not* suspect him of having an affair. If I did, I wouldn't hire someone to follow him. I'd ask him. I'd have every confidence that he'd tell me the truth." Her eyes began to brim. "Aw, shit," she mumbled.

"Mrs. Hayden—"

She snorted and wiped her nose on her sleeve. "I haven't seen Derek in ten days. What the hell is going on, anyway?"

"That's what I want to find out," I said softly.

"Why? What's your connection?"

I hesitated before answering. "It's all very speculative," I finally said. "I'd rather not get into it."

"You afraid you'll upset poor weak little old me?"

I smiled. "No, that's really not it. I just don't have very many facts to speculate with yet."

"What has he done, anyway?"

I shrugged. "Disappeared, it would seem."

"Since when is that a crime?"

"I didn't say it was a crime."

She smiled. "No, you didn't say it. Look, Mr. Coyne. I am frankly at my wits' end. Derek left for work a week ago Tuesday. Like he always does. He called me from the office, said he'd be tied up all evening. That's not unusual. Sometimes he spends the night in town. It's a long commute, and if he works too late he misses the train. So when he didn't come home, I didn't think much of it. But when he didn't call the next day, I called his office. That was on Thursday. Melanie—that's his secretary—she said he hadn't come in. And we haven't seen him since. Or heard from him." She made an exploding gesture with her hands. "Poof. Just like that. Disappeared."

"Have you notified the police?"

She flapped her hands, a gesture of frustration or confusion. "No. I—I expect to hear from him. I keep thinking today, tonight . . ."

"Maybe you should," I said quietly.

She peered at me solemnly and nodded. "Yes. I suppose you're right. He's a missing person, I guess."

"You say he drove to work," I said after an awkward silence.

"He drives to the Alewife MBTA stop. Leaves his car there and takes the subway to Park Street and walks to the office from there. I assume that's what he did that day."

"Tuesday, that was."

"Yes."

The Tuesday before the early Wednesday morning when Les Katz was struck down by a hit-and-run driver, whom I assumed was Derek Hayden. "What kind of car does your husband drive?"

"An Audi 5000. He got it just a couple of months ago. His pride and joy. Twice a week at the car wash. Changes the oil about as often as he brushes his teeth. He spent over four thousand dollars on a stereo system for it, complete with a CD player. He's earned it. He works hard. He makes a lot of money. He even got a dumb vanity plate for it."

"What's it say?"

She smiled and shook her head. "It says TARZ. That's what his buddies used to call him. It's short for Tarzan, I think, which had something to do with his aggressive way of playing basketball. Listen. I hope you can find my husband, Mr. Coyne, and I don't really care why you're looking for him. He has been acting strange, and the only thing I know about that is that it is not a reflection of our marriage. We are in good shape. I know that."

"How do you mean, strange?"

"Nervous. More late hours. More trips. I assumed it was just business pressures. He wasn't sleeping very well. He'd get up in the middle of the night and when I'd wake up and go downstairs, I'd find him sitting in the living room, no lights on, no TV or radio or anything. Just sitting there. I'd ask him what was the matter, and he'd pull me into his lap and hug me and not say anything. I mean, if he was having an affair . . ."

"Assuming he wasn't," I said.

"Assuming he wasn't, then I just don't know. Business, I suppose. Maybe Arthur could tell you."

"Concannon?"

"Yes. You know him?"

"I met him. He didn't seem very forthcoming."

"He's been very kind to me. He's as upset about this as I am, although I imagine it's more for business reasons. I've talked with him several times. He keeps asking me if I've heard from Derek."

"What about friends, relatives, anybody who might be in touch with your husband?"

She nodded. "Everybody I could think of I talked to. Trying not to upset anybody, you understand. Sort of indirect. But nobody seems to know anything."

I sat back and sighed. "Strange," I said.

She nodded. "Want more coffee?"

I shook my head. "No, thanks. Look, Mrs. Hayden—"

"Why don't you call me Brenda. I mean, I've shared all these deep, dark secrets with you."

"Fine. And I'm Brady, then."

She combed a wisp of hair away from her forehead with her fingers. "What do you want me to do?"

"I don't know. Call me if you hear from Derek. Or have him call me."

"Sure. Okay."

"Otherwise . . ."

"The girls are very confused. I don't know what to tell them."

"The truth, I guess."

She nodded. "Yes. That's what I've done. They remain confused."

"How old are your daughters?"

"Eleven and eight. Their father dotes on them. Bought them a pony. They seem to miss him very much. They're spending the weekend with their grandparents. As for me, to tell you the truth, I'm almost getting used to it. Isn't that odd? It's not even been two weeks, and I'm getting into this pattern. Except at night, I just do my chores, live my life, and don't think too much about old Tarz. It gets lonely at night."

I pushed myself away from the table and stood up. Brenda

rose and came around the table. We walked to the door. "You should report him missing," I said.

She nodded. "I guess you're right. It just makes it seem—ominous, I guess."

I opened the door. "You'll call me?"

"Yes. And you call me, too, okay?"

"If I learn anything," I said.

"Please."

I climbed into my car and pointed it at the city. As I drove, I tried to figure out what I had learned. Les Katz had been hired by Hayden's wife to follow him. Les described the wife as a blond Farrah Fawcett look-alike. Then Les was run down and killed, and Hayden disappeared.

Hayden's wife denied hiring Les. And she looked nothing like Les's description of her.

It was all very confusing. I slid a Sibelius symphony into the tape deck as I drove and decided not to try to ponder what was, for the time being, imponderable.

Route 2 heading east from Harvard circles a rotary in Concord at the prison that, when I was growing up, we called the Concord Reformatory but now has been upgraded to a Massachusetts Correctional Institution. Through several traffic lights, a sharp right angle up a hill through Lincoln, over Route 128, and then a long, wide stretch of eight-lane highway to Cambridge. From the top of the hill in Belmont, the city of Boston lay spread out before me, sharp and clear in the smogless January air. I saw the Prudential and the John Hancock and the lesser spires, steeples, towers, and smoke-stacks, and I was able to locate with precision where my office building stood in Copley Square. It was a place to go on this Saturday when there was nowhere to cast for trout or swat around a Maxfli. In my searching for Derek Hayden, I had neglected my deskwork, which would surely put Julie into a foul mood, since she tended to take that stuff very seriously. I'd clean up my desk and earn myself a peck on the cheek Monday morning when she came to work.

As Route 2 funneled toward the complex intersection at the Arlington-Cambridge line, the great new concrete MBTA station loomed, a uniquely anomalous mixture of formlessness and function. The Alewife station, where Derek Hayden habitually parked his new Audi 5000.

Why not? I thought. I turned in, took my ticket from the machine, and began my tour of the parking garage. Slots were at a premium, even on a non-commuter Saturday. I looked for an Audi 5000, license plate TARZ—color unknown, thanks to my stupid failure to ask.

It turned out to be dark metallic blue. It was on the fourth level. I found a slot nearby, parked my BMW, and strode over to Derek Hayden's pride and joy.

I circled it slowly, bending to examine the right front bumper and fender that, as I reconstructed Les Katz's fatal collision, had to have been the point of impact. I found no dent, no scratch, no broken headlight, no evidence of recent repair or touch-up.

Brenda told me that Derek kept his automobile spotlessly clean. But this one was coated with a uniform film of fine gray dust. It had been sitting there for some time. Ten days? I didn't know how to judge that.

I went back and sat in my own car. Slowly but inexorably my nicely wrought scenario was coming unraveled. Derek Hayden's wife didn't hire Les Katz. Hayden didn't run over Les, at least not in his own car. Nor did he flee with his lady friend, again, at least not in his beloved Audi.

Okay. Brenda Hayden might have lied to me. Why shouldn't she lie to a stranger? And Les I knew to be a satyr and prone to exaggeration to the point of outright mendacity. It would have been entirely in character for him to describe Brenda Hayden in wildly distorted terms on the mistaken assumption that it would impress me. And Hayden could have run down Les with somebody else's car. The girlfriend's, perhaps. And hers could have been the one they then used to flee in, leaving the Audi behind. That would serve as a neat diversion when it was eventually found.

I started up my BMW and followed the exit signs out of the parking garage.

The most likely scenario, I realized as I joined the solid

stream of shopping traffic in the Fresh Pond bottleneck, was much simpler and therefore more elegant. Les Katz had been run over by a drunk who didn't know him. Derek Hayden had nothing to do with it. A random event, nothing more. Most of them are. That was the way the world basically turned.

The question that continued to nag was this one: What had happened to Derek Hayden?

# 10

I skipped lunch and spent Saturday afternoon at my desk. I was working on a tricky separation agreement involving the division of a priceless collection of Indian artifacts the couple had accumulated during the twenty-two years of their marriage. Neither party wanted to split it. Neither would agree to selling it, either to a third party or to each other. Neither would consider a trade-off allowing the other to keep the whole thing.

My job was to get the whole thing for the husband. I talked to the wife's lawyer. His job was to get the whole thing for her. We agreed that we needed to do something creative, so we made a date to get all the parties together to try once again to hammer it out. We speculated on how F. Lee Bailey would have handled it. We concluded that one of our clients would have to murder the other for us to achieve a breakthrough.

It was nearly five when I finally got home. I was building a bourbon old-fashioned when the phone rang. It was Becca Katz.

"I haven't heard from you for a long time," she said. It

was neither a complaint nor an accusation, the way she said it. Nevertheless, I felt a sharp wince of guilt, as I had consciously been avoiding her since the evening we ended up in the bed she had previous shared with Les.

"I've been awfully busy," I said. It sounded lame. "Anyhow, there's been nothing much to report." That was an outright lie. "Well," I amended, "until just today, that is."

"What have you learned?"

"I'm not sure. It's complicated. Perhaps when I can sort it all out . . ."

"Brady, I've gathered together some of Les's things. I was hoping . . ."

Her voice trailed off. I knew what I was supposed to say. "I'll drop by sometime," I said breezily. "Nothing that demands immediate attention, I trust."

She was silent for so long that I began to feel uncomfortable. "Becca, look," I said.

Her voice was soft. "Didn't it mean anything to you?"

"It was—unexpected, I guess," I said carefully. "I don't normally, ah, jump into bed with bereaved widow ladies. It meant something, yes, It's just that—"

"You're feeling guilty."

"No, that's not it."

"You don't know what it meant to me, then. We never talked about it. You think it commits you."

"Becca—"

"You're worried that you took advantage of me, my grief, my—the fact that with Les—that I was vulnerable and didn't know what I was doing."

"Something like that, maybe."

"Well, it's all kind of true. It was unlike me. To do that. To let that happen. To *want* it to happen. But listen. I have no regrets. It was—it was therapeutic, okay? It helped me to start healing. I mean, death is hard. You want to affirm something, to feel something profound and good. Am I making too much of this? You don't have to tell me I'm the love of your life. That's not what I'm after."

"A momentary stay against confusion," I said, quoting Frost.

"Yes. Exactly."

"It was the same for me, Becca. An affirmation. It wasn't something that you did to me, or vice versa. It happened because we wanted it to. You just have to know that I'm not really available. I don't mean to you. I mean generally, to anybody. It's the way I am. It's taken me a long time to learn that about myself. It makes me cautious."

"I know that. You didn't fool me. That was part of it. You were—you are safe that way."

I lit a cigarette and sipped my old-fashioned. "Therefore, what?" I said.

"Therefore," she said promptly. "I have four lamb chops and an appetite for only two of them."

"There's a problem."

I heard her laugh softly. "You've got to forgive me. I'm not very good at this. Of course you're busy. It's Saturday night. Sometime when you have a chance, though, please drop by and pick up Les's stuff."

"That's not what I was going to say, Becca."

"Oh?"

"What I was going to say was that I like my lamb chops rare. Nothing irritates me more than overdone chops. I am very particular about rare lamb chops."

"Boy, you really know how to put the pressure on a woman, Brady Coyne."

"It'll take me an hour, at least."

"I'm waiting."

I took my glass into the bathroom, stripped down, showered, shaved, and got dressed. I found myself humming a tune from *My Fair Lady*. Something about how regrettable it is that women can't be more like men. Most of the words eluded my memory.

I arrived at Becca's place a little before seven. I rang the doorbell and waited, clutching the claret that the guy at the liquor store promised me was "spunky." I tried to imagine how Becca would look. I realized that I had trouble picturing her, this woman I had bedded a little more than a week earlier. I was able to see her eyes. The rest was a blur. And the eyes appeared to be crying.

I heard her clip-clop down the inside stairs. The door handle rattled and then opened. Becca smiled at me. She looked me up and down. Then she said, "Boy, that's a relief."

"What is?"

"That you wore your jeans. I had this panicky feeling you'd show up in a jacket and tie or something, and here I am . . ."

She twirled around. She was wearing blue jeans herself, with an orange turtleneck jersey. Both fit snugly. "You look terrific," I said sincerely.

"Well, I put on these heels, which makes me feel like a lady of the night. Isn't that what the Combat Zone hookers wear—tight pants and spike heels?"

"You don't look like a lady of the night, Becca."

"Oh," she said. "That's disappointing."

She took my hand and led me upstairs. The little dining table was spread with a blue cloth. A single candle burned in a simple pewter holder.

I gave her the wine. "I was promised this would complement, but never overpower, rare lamb chops."

She put her hand on my cheek and tiptoed up to kiss me on the chin. I gave her an awkward one-armed hug. She stepped back and smiled. "This is uncomfortable for you, isn't it?"

I shrugged and grinned.

"Don't worry about it," she said. "No demands. Why don't you make yourself a drink and I'll slide those chops under the broiler and toss the salad. I left Les's papers in that big attaché case in the living room, if you want to look at them."

I found the bottle of Early Times in the cabinet, diminished not a millimeter since I had last poured from it. Becca was working over a big wooden salad bowl, whistling and nipping at a glass of white wine.

As I left the room, she looked at me over her shoulder and

smiled. She was acting very much like a woman who expected to be loved. The idea was becoming less and less unacceptable to me.

She had stuffed the square leather attaché case with an eclectic assortment of papers—insurance polices, automobile titles, records of bank accounts, old tax forms. Personal stuff as well as business stuff. I shuffled through them distractedly. There appeared to be no will, a complication that I could deal with.

When Becca called me to the table, I shoved all the documents back into the attaché case. I'd bring them to the office and turn them over to Julie, who would organize them, make some preliminary phone calls, and arrange a session with the good folks at probate.

The lamb chops were pink and moist and accented perfectly with a hint of garlic. The baby boiled potatoes were buttered and sprinkled with flakes of parsley. The green beans were fresh, cooked al dente. There were chunks of artichoke hearts and avocado in the salad. The claret wasn't bad.

Becca told me she had been job-hunting. "The market for middle-aged English teachers who have been out of the classroom for ten years is pretty bearish," she said. "I've put my name in for substitute work."

"I can imagine nothing more depressing."

She shook her head and frowned. "I've got to get out of this place," she said. "Les never said I couldn't work, but he didn't encourage me, either. I kept planning to do something. It just never happened. Another one of those things that didn't help my self-esteem."

"I'll bet you were a good teacher."

"I enjoyed the kids and hated the bureaucracy. I was younger then. Now, I don't know."

"It's not exactly like you're over the hill, Becca."

"In some ways, I have barely started to climb the hill, sir."

I decided she intended something suggestive by that.

"So," she said after a few moments of comfortable silence, "are you going to tell me about Les's killer, or what?"

"Last night at this time, I knew who it was. I matched a picture with a name, found out where he worked. Now—I don't know again." I proceeded to fill her in on my detective work with Derek Hayden—the visit to his office, my journey to his farmhouse in Harvard, my encounter with Brenda Hayden, my discovery of Hayden's Audi in the Alewife parking garage. Becca studied my face intently as I talked. When I finished, I shrugged and spread my hands. "So I feel as if I'm back at square one," I said.

"The pictures, that reminds me," she said. "I found Les's camera. The one with the big lens that he used for his snooping."

"Where was it?"

"In his car. It's been parked right out front all this time, but when it snowed the other night I had to move it. The camera was on the floor on the passenger side. Amazing it didn't get ripped off in this neighborhood."

"As if Les had been taking pictures that night—"

"The night he got killed," she finished for me. "I never thought of that. But it makes sense. He was out in his car. Working, unless he was shacked up with somebody. If he was working, that would explain the camera being in the car."

"Why don't you get it for me."

She said, "Okay," and got up from the table. She was back a minute later, carrying in both hands a Canon SLR thirty-five-millimeter camera with a lens about a foot long. The meter showed that twenty-four frames had been exposed. I rewound the film, opened up the camera, removed the little cylinder of film, and deposited it in my pants pocket. Then I handed the camera back to her.

"I can get this developed," I said, thinking of Gloria with another confusion of emotions.

"You think he might've been taking pictures at night?"

I took out the cassette of Fuji film and looked at it. "It's possible. This is a very fast film he was using. Twelve-hundred speed. It would certainly work indoors. Maybe even in city lights. We'll see."

Becca began to carry the dishes into the kitchen. I got up and helped her. When the table was cleared, she said, "Let's just leave them in the sink. I'll load up the dishwasher later. It's time for a little brandy."

I got the bottle and she found two round snifters. We toted them into the living room and placed them on the glass-topped coffee table in front of the sofa. She sat on the sofa. I sat beside her and poured a finger of brandy into each snifter. We lifted them, cupping them in the palms of our hands in the approved fashion. We sipped without the preliminary of a toast. Becca placed her glass on the table and turned to face me. "Ready?" she said.

Later I lay on my back staring up into the darkness of Becca's bedroom. Her cheek rested on my shoulder. I could feel her warm breath on my chest and the gentle rise and fall of her breast as she breathed.

We lay in silence for a long time. I assumed she was sleeping. Then she whispered, "Brady?"

I twisted my head and kissed her hair. "I'm here."

"I was thinking."

"Dangerous, thinking. I order you to stop instantly."

She hitched herself up in the bed. I adjusted myself so that she could lean back against me. "No, really," she said. "I was thinking about Les."

"Terrific."

She laughed softly. "Not like that, dummy. I was thinking about how he decided to become a detective, and what if things had been different. You know, how your mind sort of goes off in weird directions when you're totally relaxed and half asleep?"

"Mmm," I said.

"Did he ever tell you?"

"Tell me what?"

"How he became a detective?"

"No. He never did."

"It was at a bridge tournament. I'm surprised he never told you. He loved to tell the story."

"We mostly just talked business, Becca." I stroked her flank. I wanted her to stop talking. Instead she sat upright.

"He suspected this pair of cheating. I guess they were making some unusual leads or something, and Les figured there was no way they would do what they did unless they had found some illegal way to communicate. What I really think was that they beat Les and his partner, and he didn't think they were that good. You know Les. He never lacked self-esteem."

"For sure," I said, declining to tell her that I really didn't know Les that well.

"Anyway," she continued, her hand resting idly on my leg, "he knew this pair was going to compete in another tournament the next week, so he spoke to the director and told him what he suspected. The director arranged it so Les could keep an eye on them. Everyone at those tournaments knew Les, so his hanging around didn't arouse any suspicions. About halfway through the first day of the tournament, Les went to the director and said, 'If East leads a heart, I can tell you how they're doing it.' I can still hear Les telling it. He could tell it better than me. Anyway, East did lead a heart. His partner had a void in hearts, so he trumped it, which set the contract. There was nothing in the bidding to suggest a heart lead. Do you understand bridge, Brady?"

"I play now and then. I have trouble keeping partners."

"Because you're not very good?"

"No. Because I'm too critical. It's a character flaw. Bridge brings it out. Nothing else does. So I don't play too often, and I don't play with friends."

Becca laughed quickly. "It's a common malady," she said. "There are lots of ways to cheat at bridge. Lots of people do it. In tournaments it's harder. People've tried voice cues in their bidding, hesitations, subtle inflections. There are ways of holding the cards. Finger cues. Body language. Some of it really clever. But most opponents are very alert to stuff like this. Which is why there's very little cheating. This pair had a new way. It turns out that West was wearing this diamond ring on his right pinkie. Whenever they were defending a hand, if he wanted a heart lead he'd turn the ring around so that the stone wasn't showing. And, of course not turning the ring around told his partner not to lead a heart. Information like that makes winners out of average players in tournament bridge. And Les was the only one to pick it up. He liked to say that nailing those two cheats was ten times the kick of playing bridge. After that, he gradually quit playing professionally and started hiring out as a sort of troubleshooter at the tournaments. He exposed a few more cheats, and one time he caught a woman who was stealing from the rooms of the hotel where the tournament was being held."

She fell silent. After a moment she turned and hugged me. There was a panicky, violent quality to her embrace. I could feel her nails dig into my shoulders. "Hey, Becca," I whispered.

"I'm okay," she said. "Just let me hold on to you."

It was a minute before I realized she was crying. I caressed her ineffectually, rubbing my hand in circles on her back.

"I was thinking," she said, sniffing. "If it hadn't been for that void in hearts, everything would be different. I mean, if Les had been wrong, he'd probably still be a bridge pro. Writing columns. Winning master points for LOL's. He'd probably still be alive. And I never would have met him. And I wouldn't have met you. And—but that's dumb, huh?"

I stroked her hair. "Kinda dumb."

She snuffled and then laughed softly. "Anyway, there wasn't that much work for a detective who specialized in bridge cheats. But Les really liked snooping around, I guess. Oh, he was a sweet man, in his way. But he had this funny part of him. He used to say about those card cheats, he'd say, 'Nothing I hate worse than cheats.' I mean, that's ironic as hell, since he used to cheat on me emotionally. But he was very up front about it, which to him meant he wasn't cheating at all. Anyway, he thought cheating at cards was the worst."

Her hand began to rub my chest. She squirmed around and kissed my throat. "I'm sorry to talk about Les," she mumbled.

"It's okay." I touched her chin and she tilted her face up.

Her eyes glittered in the darkness, and although I knew it was only tears, there was a feral, predatory look on her face that made me hesitate before I kissed her. Then she moved against me and groaned, and I pulled her on top of me so she could follow me down the dark tunnel into brief but blessed oblivion.

Becca slept fetally, with her knees drawn up toward her chest and her hands squeezed between them. Her velvet-smooth rump was thrust back against the curve of my body. My face was in her hair. It smelled like the breeze after a spring rainstorm. Her head lay across my upper arm, which had gone tingly while I dozed.

I gently drew my body back from hers. She stirred and wiggled against me. I slid my arm free, stroked her shoulder, and eased myself out of her bed. I dressed in the darkness and felt my way into the living room, where I had left my shoes.

When I was ready to leave, I went back into the bedroom. I bent to kiss her. Her eyes were wide open. "You have to go?"

I kissed her forehead. "Yes."

The light that entered from the bedroom windows allowed me to see her smile. "What time is it?" she said.

"A little after four."

Her bare arm snaked out from under the covers, touched my jaw, then hooked around my neck, drawing my face down to hers. Her mouth opened under mine. It was she who broke away from the kiss. I straightened up. "I know," she said. "You're not available."

"Becca—"

"Shh," she said. "It's okay. It's just right. Keep in touch, Brady."

I touched her hair. "I will. I promise."

A pale line had begun to show on the ocean's horizon as I stood by the sliding glass doors of my apartment. I watched the line expand as the earth resolutely rotated to face the sun.

Pale swatches of yellow brushed themselves onto the under-side of the bank of cumulus clouds over the horizon, trans-forming them as I watched into gold, then to orange. The promise of a fair winter's day.

The appearance of the arc of the sun was sudden, heralded by a startling flash of light. Daybreak happened literally—an instantaneous break from dark to light, from night to day.

I had dozed only fitfully for a few hours with Becca Katz. Our lovemaking had agitated my system, so that while she slumped easily into deep, peaceful sleep, I fidgeted and squirmed, my mind darting and twisting through mazes of half-real images and concepts that seemed at once brilliant and outrageous. Now I stood at the instant of a new Sunday, too exhausted to pursue any ambition but too wakeful to go to bed.

So I did the logical things: I fed Mr. Coffee and switched him on, and then I took a shower.

By the time I emerged, the coffee was ready. I sat with a big mug at the table by the windows. The lower curve of the sun had cleared the Atlantic. The sky was brilliant blue, the ocean a cold, angry gray-green. I checked my watch. Quarter of seven. Still too early to call Gloria. So I made some toast, plastered it with peanut butter, and consumed it between sips of coffee.

Another culinary triumph from the kitchen of Brady L. Coyne.

Finally, at seven-thirty, I dialed Gloria's number. She answered on the third ring with a mumbled, "Hmmm?"

"I thought you'd be awake. It's a gorgeous day. Crisp, bright, gorgeous. The sunrise was spectacular."

"Oh. It's you."

"Cock-a-doodle-doo."

"Brady, for Christ's sake, what time is it?"

"Seven-thirty, Gloria. Already you've missed the best part of the day."

"So what the hell are you so cheerful about?"

Becca Katz, I thought. She knows how to cook lamb chops. She loves me a little. But not too much. She hums in her sleep. There's a gentle, vulnerable roundness of stomach, a soft, inviting slope of hip. "Don't accuse me of being cheerful," I said sternly.

She sighed. "So much for sleeping in. Joey's off on a ski weekend, hellbent on getting drunk and knocking up Ruthie McAllister, probably. So I thought I'd just do a lazy Sunday morning for myself." She hesitated, then said quietly, "Like we used to."

"When we were much younger," I said. "The Sunday *Times*, croissants, and fresh-squeezed orange juice. Gallons of coffee."

"And a little hanky-panky under the sheets."

"That was all before we had kids."

"That," said Gloria, "was all before we got married."

I felt my joie de vivre draining away, as if someone had yanked out a plug in the bottom of my stomach. "The reason I called—"

"The weather report, I assumed. To annoy me."

"No, I've got another roll of film that needs developing. Any chance . . . ?"

"Today, you mean?"

"The sooner the better. It's kind of urgent."

"You still playing detective?"

"Sort of. What do you say?"

She sighed. "There's no one here to bring me croissants anyway. It's not the same if you have to go downstairs and get them yourself. I might as well get up. Come on over. I'll put the coffee on."

"Thanks, hon."

"I wish you wouldn't say that."

"Say what?"

"Hon. It's not fair."

I was halfway to Wellesley when I remembered Les Katz's suitcase-size attaché crammed with the documents I would need to settle his estate. It was still in Becca's living room, on the floor beside the soft chair where I left it when I slipped away in the dark.

Forgetting it, I supposed, was one of those purposeful accidents Freud loved to analyze. I'd just have to go back and retrieve it someday soon.

# 11

"Are you going to church?" I said to Gloria when she came to the door. She was wearing a calf-length wool skirt, a white blouse with a good deal of lace and frill at the throat, a maroon jacket, and high leather boots.

She looked smashing.

"I don't go to church anymore," she said with a smile. "You cured me of that a long time ago."

"A business meeting, then," I said as I followed her into the house. "I'm interfering."

"You're not interfering." She took my parka and tossed it on a chair. We went downstairs.

I fished the roll of film out of my pocket and handed it to her. She looked at it. "Twelve-hundred. There won't be much quality to this," she observed.

"I'm not interested in quality. I just want to know what's on it."

"Well, let's find out, then."

She took off her jacket and slipped into an apron that was hanging on a hook beside the door to her darkroom. Then she went in, leaving me with her photography magazines. I riffled absentmindedly through them, first sitting, and then adjusting myself so that I was lying on the sofa. After a few minutes, I dropped the magazine onto the floor and allowed my eyes to close.

I realized that Gloria had never answered my question. Was it a business meeting? Or did she get all dressed up for me?

Was it any of my business?

"Hey, there." Her voice came from far away. Her hand was on my cheek, first stroking and then gently slapping. "Come on, big guy. Rise and shine."

She was seated on the sofa, her rump against my hip, looking down at me.

"Must've dozed off," I mumbled.

"The neighbors have been complaining about your snoring," she said, smiling.

I craned my neck, then put my hand on it. "I shouldn't have slept that way," I said. "Got a stiff neck."

"Sit up," she said. I did. She went around behind me and placed both of her hands on my neck. She poked and probed, working at the hard muscles and tendons, from just behind my ears down to my shoulders, her thumbs strong and insistent. I arched against her massage.

"Mmm," I said with a groan. "You should've been a masseuse. Preferably topless. Nobody can do that like you."

"Nobody can do lots of things like me."

I reached behind me, got my arm around her neck, and pulled her onto my lap. "Hey," she said softly. But she allowed herself to be drawn down so that she sat on me. She ducked down and burrowed her face into my shoulder. I touched her chin with my forefinger, urging her to look at me. When she did, she was frowning.

"You must've had a late night, to conk off like that."

"I didn't sleep well."

"I understand." She twisted her face away.

I put my fingers in her hair and made her face me. "Gloria," I said.

"Please don't."

Her lips were unyielding, her eyes wide open and staring myopically into mine. I pulled back from the one-sided kiss. "Sorry," I said.

"I wish you'd make up your mind."

I nodded. "Me, too."

"You can't have it all, you know."

"I guess I don't know that."

She smiled. "You're impossible."

"I'm difficult. I'm improbable. But I'm not impossible. I'm very possible."

She shook her head slowly. She moved her face close to mine. She hesitated, then, abruptly, she stood up. She smoothed her skirt against the fronts of her thighs. "Jesus!" she breathed.

"I'm sorry, hon."

"This is a recording."

"Ever notice how we do so much better by phone?"

She nodded. Her look was solemn. "Brady, I've got a date this afternoon."

"A date."

"Yes. A real live date. And guess what? He's—ready?—he's a lawyer."

"Anyone I know?"

"I don't know. I don't think I'll tell you his name. If you know him, you'll just tell me why he's wrong for me."

"Would I do that?"

"You bet your ass you would."

"Is he married?"

"What's it to you?"

"Absolutely nothing."

"Well, I'm not going to tell you that, either."

She turned away from me and bent to pick up the magazine I had dropped onto the floor. She put the magazine on the table and made a show of arranging the stack into neat, chronological order. Without turning back to face me, she said, "Do you love all the ladies you date?"

"In some ways I do. It's all sort of relative."

"I'm just starting to learn that. For a long time I thought

there's no sense in risking a relationship with someone you're not sure you're going to love. So I found myself saying no thank you to men I liked well enough. And then it began to occur to me that just because I didn't love them the way—you know—the way I used to, the way I know I can, it didn't mean I couldn't—couldn't go out with them.''

"Go out with them," I repeated. "A euphemism, huh?"

She turned to face me. She nodded. "Yes. A euphemism."

I cleared my throat. "I see."

"Brady, for God's sake. It was you who told me I was so stuck in the old double standard that I had lost my identity. I mean, that was what our divorce was all about, if I remember correctly. But the thing is, it's you who's got the double standard problem."

"I just don't want you to be hurt."

"You don't want me to get laid."

"Jesus, Gloria."

"Hey," she said, laughing now. "If you don't want me to be hurt, don't come on to me. Don't tease me. And for Christ's sake, don't judge me. You think after eight years I shouldn't go out with men?"

"I don't know. None of my business anyway. Forget it. Be happy, if you can."

"I'm trying."

I stood up and went to her. I opened my arms and she came to me. I hugged her and kissed her hair. "I *am* sorry," I said. "Can we be friends?"

She leaned back so she could look up at me. "I seriously doubt it," she said. She stepped back. "Do you want to see those pictures?"

I nodded. She led me to her darkroom. "I made a contact sheet first," she said. "There were twenty-four exposures. The first twelve of them were so badly underexposed that you couldn't see a thing. Then there were five where you can make something out. Whoever took them was playing with f-stops and shutter speeds. The five that came out at all are still pretty bad. Wide-open lens, maybe a sixtieth of a second, maybe even slower. Very shallow focus, lots of tremor. Using a long lens, I'd guess. And film that fast just doesn't get you much quality under the best conditions. Anyhow, I made enlargements of the five that showed something.''

The five prints were laid out side by side. "Are they in order?" I asked Gloria.

She nodded. "He was bracketing them. There were some in between these that didn't come out. But this is the sequence in which he took them, left to right.''

They were all taken at night outside somewhere on a roadside. In the background were the blurry lights of what appeared to be a storefront. All of the pictures were of a man and an automobile. Most of the light came from the storefront, so that the figures in the picture appeared almost as silhouettes. The car's lights were on. In the first three frames, the man was leaning over to peer in through the passenger's window, evidently talking with whoever was inside the car. Although his face was a shadow, and even realizing that I might be imagining it, the figure appeared to be Derek Hayden.

The fourth frame showed Hayden, if that's who it was, entering the car.

The fifth was of the automobile itself. It was in a different position from the previous frames, suggesting it was pulling away from the curb.

"Do you have a magnifying glass?" I said to Gloria.

"Sure.'' She handed it to me. I examined each photograph. I concluded that, unlike the previous set of shots Gloria had developed and printed for me, these offered no clues as to location. The backgrounds were composed of blurry shapes and spots of white. One of the photos showed the man in fairly sharp profile, deepening my conviction that it was Derek Hayden.

The last photo, even less well focused than the previous four, interested me the most. It showed the license plate from the rear, dimly illuminated by the light over it.

"See if you can read that number," I said, pointing at the license.

Gloria took the glass from me. "One, five—the third digit is either a two or a zero. Let's see. That's a seven, zero, and either a four or an eight." She handed the glass to me. "You try."

I had written down the numbers as Gloria read them to me. I pushed the pencil and paper at her. "You write what I say, now," I told her.

I studied it through the glass. I was less certain about a couple more digits than Gloria had been, so we looked together and finally agreed on four of them. The last one, which Gloria thought was either a four or an eight, looked like a blob to me no matter what she said.

"What kind of car is it?" she said.

I shrugged. "Squarish. Midsize. It's just part of a shape. If I can trace the license number, I won't need to know the make of the car."

"How are you going to do that?"

"Charlie."

"How is old Charlie?"

"He still can't beat me at golf. That pisses him off. Otherwise, he's fine."

She glanced at her wristwatch. "Well," she said.

I nodded. "You've got a date. You'd just as soon I wasn't here when he arrived."

"He's not coming here. I'm meeting him."

"How very twentieth-century of you."

"Sometimes I even call him on the phone."

"What would your mother say?"

"The same thing she said when she found out you and I were sleeping together in New Haven."

"She said, as I recall," I said, " 'just as long as you plan to marry the young man.' "

She grinned. "Which, in this case, I am not planning to do. So I'm not telling her."

"Perhaps I'll give her an anonymous phone call."

She punched my shoulder. "Don't you dare."

Gloria and I exchanged pecks on the cheek at the door,

and I walked out to my car. I had the photographs in an envelope under my arm.

As I backed out of the driveway, I saw Gloria standing behind the storm door. She had her hand raised, her palm pressed flat against the glass.

I called Charlie McDevitt on Monday morning. When he came on the line, he said, "You still hanging on to that stick of dynamite?"

"One in each hand," I said. "The fuses are burning down."

"You want to talk about it?" I detected sincere concern in his voice.

"Charlie, you are a good guy, no matter what everybody says. I appreciate you. But I can handle it."

He chuckled. "Right, counselor."

"Anyway, I need a favor."

"*Another* favor, you mean."

"Right. I stand corrected. Can you use your considerable clout with the Registry of Motor Vehicles to trace a license for me?"

"Nobody, my friend, has considerable clout with the Registry. They are collectively the most arrogant collection of sons and daughters of bitches—"

"Shit," I said. "You mean—?"

"I mean, I'll use my considerable clout with the state police, if it's all the same to you."

"It's all the same. Here's the number." I read him the digits Gloria and I had interpreted from the photograph. "One, five, something, seven, zero, something?"

"What the hell are those 'somethings'?"

"The first something could be a two or a zero. Something that looks round. The terminal something might be eight. Or four. Or three."

Charlie's sigh hissed in my ear. "My clout may be considerable," he said. "But it ain't unlimited."

"Can't they just ask their computers?"

"Sure. But a six-digit plate with two unknowns gives the possibility of one hundred different numbers."

"You are quick, mathematically."

"I am quick in several respects, some of them unfortunate."

"A list of a hundred would help me."

"Brady, you already owe me one lunch."

"We can upgrade that one. Or we can make it two."

"I'll give it serious thought. I'll call you when I've got something for you."

It was Tuesday afternoon before he got back to me. "Their computers were down for a while," he said. "And they seem to have strange priorities over there. Murders, shit like that, they like to work on. My friend was more than a little aggravated when he realized there were two unknowns in that license number. Now it turns out I've gotta buy him a lunch."

"Hey, I'll take you both to lunch. Place of your choosing."

"Just so you understand."

"I understand."

"He sent a cop over with the printout. Two solid pages, single-spaced. Eighty-seven numbers, with names and addresses. I guess the other thirteen possibilities aren't in use."

"I'll be right over."

I grabbed my coat and went out to stand beside Julie, who was on the telephone. She glanced up at me, scowled her automatic disapproval, which seems to be the one predictable response I can instantly arouse in a woman, and then returned to her conversation. It consisted mostly of her listening and injecting a "certainly" or "of course" here and there into the available spaces. When she hung up, she said, "That was Mr. Barth. Complaining about having to go to another meeting with his wife. He wants you to take care of it."

"How'd you leave it? He's really got to be there."

She grinned. "Oh, he'll be there. He's really hung up on those arrowheads."

"Did you leave him smiling?"

"Of course."

"How'd you manage that?"

"I agreed with him."

"On what?"

"He said he guessed you weren't competent to handle it by yourself."

"Gee, thanks."

"Now where are you off to?"

"Gotta go see Charlie McDevitt. Why don't you hand out the Gone Fishin' sign and go home?"

"Somebody's got to watch the shop, Brady. What's up with Mr. McDevitt? You two poring over brochures about fishing for Arctic char in Newfoundland?"

"It happens to be business," I sniffed.

It took me at least ten frigid minutes to persuade a cab to stop for me and another several to persuade the hack to understand my destination. He was swarthy and full-bearded, and all he said to me was, "Yah?" along with a number of incoherent mutterings, and he said them in a distinctly foreign accent. Something Middle Eastern, I guessed. Boylston Street was jammed. Charles Street was a mess. It took nearly half an hour to get to Charlie's office. I paid the cabbie, and when I waved away the change he tried to give me, he said something that sounded like, "Gubba malloon." His broad, yellow-toothed grin told me he was pleased and would love to drive me someplace else.

Charlie is a demonstrative Irishman. He hugged me when I entered his office and offered me a shot of Old Rubber Boot. I accepted. He slid the computer printout to me while he went to the cabinet where he hid his booze. By the time he returned to his chair at the desk with a bottle and measured out two glasses of amber liquid, I had scanned the list.

I accepted the glass from him. "Thanks anyway," I said.

"No help?"

I folded the printout and shoved it into my pocket. Then I tilted back my head and downed the shot of bourbon. I held my glass to Charlie. He took it and poured in another two fingers. This I decided to sip.

"That," he said, "does not excuse you from your obligation, you know."

"Lunch for you and your pal over on Commonwealth Avenue."

"We were thinking the Café Budapest."

"Whatever. That's a nice place."

"Expensive. We wanted something expensive. My pal has this attitude toward lawyers."

I shrugged. "It's our cross."

Charlie leaned toward me. "You're really hung up on this lady, huh?"

I shook my head. "That's not it. I just thought I had a handle on what happened to Les Katz. But none of the facts seem to fit."

He nodded. "You do tend to go off chasing windmills, friend."

"I'm aware of that. The thing is, these windmills don't even turn out to be windmills. Nothing but mirage and illusion. It's discouraging."

"In that case," said Charlie, "there's only one thing to do."

"And what is that?"

He lifted the bottle. "Have another."

# 12

Thursday night. The eleven o'clock news was all good, if one is willing to discount continued strife in the Middle East and layoffs at the Framingham General Motors plant. The blizzard that paralyzed Chicago didn't strike me as bad news at all, nor did Larry Bird's backache or a caustic review of Robert Redford's recent film.

I flicked off the television, stretched and yawned, and was on my way to brush my teeth when the phone rang.

I detoured to the bedroom, flopped on my bed, and picked up the receiver. "Coyne," I said.

I heard labored breathing.

"Hello?" I said. "Who is this?"

"Oh, Brady . . ." The voice sounded far away.

"Becca? Is that you?"

"Yes. Oh, God . . ."

"Hey, take it easy. What's the matter?"

"I told him. I didn't want to. I'm sorry. But I told him."

"Who? You told who what? Becca, what is going on?"

"Brady, please . . ."

"Do you want me to come over?"

She was crying softly.

"Becca?"

"Yes. Please come. Oh, please."

"I'm on my way."

I pulled up in front of her house twenty minutes later, having violated about a dozen traffic regulations along the way. The light was on over her front door. I jabbed at the bell and instantly heard the upstairs door creak. A moment later Becca unlocked the door that opened onto the porch where I stood. She wore a big bulky robe with the collar turned up around her ears. I bent to kiss her, but she drew away from me and averted her face. She turned and trudged up the stairs into her apartment. She moved painfully. I followed her.

She led me into her living room. A small table had been knocked over and the rug was mussed up. The sofa had been shoved backward.

Becca sat on the sofa, her head dipped into her hands. She began to cry.

I sat beside her and put my arm across her shoulders. "What can I get you?"

"Just hold me for a minute."

So I did. She turned to me and burrowed her face into my chest. She rested her hands lightly on my hips. She kept her body bent away from contact with me. I stroked her back and said nothing. After a few minutes she shuddered and lifted her face to look at me.

"My God, Becca! What happened?"

Her left cheekbone was puffed out so that her eye was nearly closed. It was angry red. By tomorrow it would be the color of a ripe eggplant. I touched it with my forefinger and she jerked back. "It hurts," she said.

"Are you hurt anywhere else?"

She shook her head. "No. He only had to hit me once and I told him everything. I'm so sorry, Brady."

"Sit here. I'll be right back."

I went into her kitchen and dumped out a tray of ice cubes into a towel. I found a half-full bottle of chablis in the refrigerator and poured two glasses. I took the ice and the wine into the living room. I put the glasses on the coffee table and made a cumbersome compress of the ice cubes wrapped in the towel. This I placed gently against her bruised cheek. "Hold this here. It'll deaden the pain and keep the swelling down."

She obeyed. Then I handed her the wine.

She smiled lopsidedly from behind the bulky ice pack and sipped from the glass.

"Now," I said, "do you think you can talk about it?"

She nodded. "I'll try. It's not so much the pain. But I was so frightened. I thought he was going to kill me. He threatened to kill me. I—I wet my pants. I was humiliated and frightened at the same time. I would have done anything he said. I—I did what he said."

"Start from the beginning, Becca."

"Okay. I had been out shopping. I came home—it was, I don't know, maybe eight-thirty or nine o'clock. I had two big bags of groceries. I was sort of balancing them on my hip, you know, trying to find my key in my purse. Finally I put the bags down—oh, this isn't part of it. Anyway, I got the door open and I was bending down for the bags and—and that's when he grabbed me. I don't know where he came from, but he was there, right behind me, and his hand was on my mouth. It was so strong and tight I couldn't yell or anything. He shoved me inside and half carried me up the stairs. When we got inside he whispered into my ear, he said, 'If you scream I'll kill you.' He was very strong. I nodded my head. He moved his hand away from my mouth and grabbed my throat. He was waiting to see if I'd scream. I was so frightened—it was like I was paralyzed—I don't think I *could* have screamed."

She paused, sipped her wine, and removed the ice pack from her cheek. "It's numb now. It feels better," she said. I leaned toward her and kissed the ugly bruise and she tried to smile. Only one side of her face seemed to be operational.

"Anyhow," she continued, staring down at her wineglass, which she held in both hands between her knees, "he sort of half carried me into the living room—here—and shoved me at the sofa. I landed on the floor. It was the first chance I had to see him. But he was wearing this ski mask. It looked like one of those hideous African tribal masks. All weird colors and a big mouth that looked like death.''

"What else do you remember about him?"

She closed her eyes for a moment. "I was so scared . . ."

"Try."

"He seemed so big. But he was probably average height. I don't know. He had on a heavy coat. Dark color. Wool or something like that. He seemed—bulky. Heavy. Muscular. But maybe not. It's so hard. His voice was muffled behind the mask. It was deep." She shrugged. "He was a man. I guess that's about all I'm sure of.''

"What color was his skin?"

She frowned. "I don't know. I think he had gloves on. Yes. I remember his hand on my mouth. Leather gloves. His face and hands—all of his skin was covered. And his hair.'' She looked beseechingly at me. "I'm sorry."

"It's okay. Look. You've been assaulted, that much is obvious. I'm going to call the police. Wait right here.''

"Don't. Please."

"Of course I will."

"He said not to."

I hugged her. "Shh," I whispered. "He won't be back. We've got to catch him.''

I went into the kitchen and phoned the Somerville police. I gave my name and Becca's address, told the businesslike male voice I was reporting an assault, and was informed that a cruiser was in the area and would be over directly. Then I went back to Becca.

Her wineglass was empty. I refilled it and topped off my own.

"The police are on their way. Now. Tell me what happened after he brought you in here.''

"He shoved me. I told you that. I was on the floor. I started to stand up and he hit me. With his fist. Just—without warning or anything. I didn't expect it. You don't expect to get hit. He didn't ask me a question or threaten me or anything. He just slugged me. Everything went black for a minute. And then he was beside me here, on the sofa, and that nightmare face was close to mine. He said, 'Where's the camera?' I panicked. I didn't know what he was talking about, and all I could think was that he was going to hit me again. I said, 'What camera?' I tried to pull away from him, and he grabbed my hair. He said, 'Your husband's camera.' So I told him, and he went and got it. Then he came back and he grabbed my arm, here''—she touched her bicep—''and he squeezed me hard. He said, 'Where's the film that was in it?' 'Brady,' I told him. I just—I gave him your name. I was so scared. I know I shouldn't have. I had no courage.''

I stroked her hair. ''Shh. It's all right. So you told him that I had the film.''

She nodded and turned away from me. ''I'm so sorry. Yes, I gave him your name. I was crying. My legs were all wet from—from being so scared. I guess he believed me. He stood up. He didn't ask me anything else.''

''He didn't ask you who I was, where I lived, anything like that?''

''No.'' She frowned. ''I don't see—''

''Then what?''

''Then he told me not to call the police. He said not to move or he'd come back and kill me. I told him I promised. I guess he believed me. And I didn't. I waited for a long time before I called you. I kept thinking he was trying to fool me, that he was hiding somewhere to see if I'd do anything. I started to call you several times. But I was so scared. Finally I did.''

''Becca,'' I said, ''the police are going to ask you all these questions. Tell them everything you can think of. I'll be here, but I won't be able to help you. There are some things about the photographs and so forth that you don't know, or that you know only because I told you. I'll tell them about that. I'm your lawyer, remember. Tell them the truth. There's nothing to hide.''

She peered up at me. ''My lawyer?''

I shrugged. "And your friend."

She smiled and nodded.

"Can you think of anything to identify the guy?" I said after an awkward moment. "Could you see his eyes through the mask? His teeth? Did his breath smell? Any kind of accent? What he was wearing?"

She shook her head vigorously back and forth. "It's hard. When he put his face close to mine . . ." She smiled quickly. "No. That was my own urine I smelled. Before I called you, I showered. I felt so dirty. Not just from wetting myself. Dirty all over."

The doorbell rang. I went downstairs to answer it. Two policemen were standing on the porch. One of them was the young red-haired cop named Kerrigan, who had been at the hospital the day Les died. I shook hands with him.

"This is Cruikshank," he said, nodding his head toward his partner.

"Brady Coyne," I said. "The lady's lawyer."

We went upstairs. "Did you touch anything?" said Kerrigan.

"Of course. My fingerprints are all over the place. The guy was wearing gloves anyway. The room is pretty much as it was when he was here."

"What happened?"

"Mrs. Katz got beat up."

Kerrigan nodded. I led them into the living room. Kerrigan kneeled in front of Becca as she sat huddled on the sofa. "Mrs. Katz," he said gently. "Remember me?"

"Officer Kerrigan," she said softly. "Of course. I'm glad it's you."

Cruikshank stood off to the side while Kerrigan interrogated Becca. He did it in a very structured manner, and Becca's responses were concise and to the point. I was gratified that he didn't ask her anything that I neglected to think of.

As I expected, he queried both of us closely about Les's photographs, as well as the film I had taken from the camera. I did most of the talking, filling him in on my amateur detective work. As I talked, Kerrigan shook his head slowly in disbelief.

"Has Hayden's wife reported him missing?" he asked when I finished talking.

"I don't know. She hadn't when I saw her."

"And as far as you know, the car, his Audi, is still at the Alewife station?"

"It was there last Saturday."

Kerrigan was taking notes. He asked a few more questions and then snapped his notebook shut. "You'll both have to come down to the station to make a complete statement. We can wait till morning for that." He turned to his partner. "Al, you want to do down and radio this description in? Slim chance, but maybe somebody will spot the guy."

Cruikshank shrugged. "Doubtful he'll still be wearing his ski mask."

After Cruikshank left, Kerrigan gestured for me to follow him into the kitchen. When we were beyond Becca's hearing, he said, "The guy's probably long gone, but we'll stick close by."

"You think she might still be in danger?" I said.

He shook his head. "Doubt it. He got what he wanted out of her." He touched my shoulder. "You probably ought to be careful, though."

He went back into the living room and bent to pat Becca's shoulder. Then I walked down the stairs to the front door with him. "You told me the first time we met that you were a rookie," I said to him.

He nodded. "Yes."

"For what it may be worth, I think you handled this perfectly. I appreciate it."

"I told Al I should handle it, knowing Mrs. Katz and all. Normally he'd have been in charge. He's senior to me. Thing is, I'm finding out you grow up fast on this job. I'm learning a lot. Remind Mrs. Katz to lock those doors."

Kerrigan joined his partner in the cruiser that was double-parked in front of Becca's house. They sat in the front seat together for several minutes talking under the dome light. Then they pulled slowly away.

I went back up to join Becca. Her wineglass was full. It was her third, at least. "They'll be in the neighborhood all night," I told her.

She nodded, watching me.

"So I guess I'll get back home, let you sleep."

She raised her glass to her lips. "Won't you stay?"

I shrugged. "I could. I thought—"

"Please?"

I nodded. "If you'd rather. Probably best if I sleep on the sofa."

"No. I need to be held."

I smiled. "Well, okay."

She went into the bedroom, taking her wine with her. I straightened out the furniture in the living room. When I tiptoed into the darkened bedroom, Becca said, "You forgot Les's stuff the other night. When you snuck out of here."

"I didn't sneak. Where is it?"

"In his den. By the chair."

I went into the den and found the attaché case. I took it into the kitchen and put it on top of the table, where I'd be sure to see it when I left. Then I returned to the bedroom.

I undressed in the dark. Becca's breathing was slow and rhythmic. I slipped between the sheets beside her. She stirred and groaned. I eased my body against hers. She wiggled against me, sighed, and mumbled, "I love you."

I kissed her shoulder. "My God, Coyne," I said to myself. "Now what?"


I woke up early, as I always do. From Becca's bedroom window I could see the winter sky, still dark and starry. I rolled onto my stomach, but it was too late. I was awake for the day.

I eased myself out of bed and dressed quietly. Then I bent beside her. "Hey," I whispered. "Wake up for a second."

She rolled over and opened her eyes. "What?"

"How do you feel?"

"Like I've been run over by a truck." Her eyes suddenly widened. I knew what she was remembering. "Oh, Jesus," she said.

I kissed her. "Listen. I'm leaving for a few hours. I want to go home, change, get cleaned up, call my secretary. I'll be back at nine. We'll go to the police station together. I want you to get up and do all the locks behind me. Okay?"

"Do you always have to go like this?"

"Hey, I'll be right back. Come on, now."

She nodded. She got out of bed and shook herself so that her nightgown, which had been riding up over her hips while she slept, fell down around her. "You," I said to her, "are truly a sight."

Her hand went to her cheek. "I must look awful."

"On the contrary. You are very sexy."

"You could stay, you know."

"I'll be back. Promise."

I remembered to take Les's attaché case. Becca followed me down the stairs. I kissed her at the doorway. "Remember the locks," I said. "You'll be all right. Be ready by nine, okay?"

She yawned extravagantly. "Sure. Gonna get a little more sleep first. What time is it?"

"Little after five."

"Brady," she said, touching my arm. "Thank you."

"Sure, kid."

I love to drive in the darkness of early morning, when the roads are empty except for a few trucks, and no lights show in the windows of the houses, and you can get stations from Chicago and St. Louis on the car radio. Getting up at what most people consider ungodly hours makes me feel I'm getting my money's worth out of the allotted hours of my life.

I parked in my reserved slot in the parking garage in the basement of my apartment building, lifted Les's attaché case off the seat beside me, and slid out of my car.

I was halfway to the elevator when I heard the shriek of tires and the whine of an engine at high speed. I tried to throw myself sideways, but in the instant before the red explosion in my brain I heard the awful sound of glass shattering and metal crumpling, and when I failed to feel the pain I knew that it had to be bad.

# 13

I greeted the pain, when it arrived, with profound relief. But it hurt too much for me to remain grateful. It felt as if someone had driven a six-inch spike straight into my head, right through my left ear, and then commenced to wiggle it around inside.

I lay on the concrete floor of the parking garage and conducted a cautious reconnaissance of my extremities. I tried to wiggle the fingers on my left hand. I felt nothing. I tried to lift my arm so I could examine my hand. It wouldn't move. I pinched my left forearm. It felt as if it were not attached to my body. When I tried to move my head to see if my arm was in fact still affixed, pain fired in my elbow and armpit. I let my head fall back onto the cold concrete.

I gazed around the parking garage. A thick gray cloud appeared to have settled in. I discerned blurry shapes. They were revolving slowly in a counterclockwise direction. My body seemed to be revolving with them.

I heard a car door clank open, then the scrape of shoes on the floor. Then, from somewhere else in the bowels of the parking garage, came the sound of an automobile starting up. The shoes scraped quickly away and the car door chunked shut. I heard the car's engine rev and speed away. The echo reverberated long after the car was gone.

I settled into the concrete floor, which seemed as cushiony as a water bed under me. My mind drifted on the gray cloud.

Later there were voices, engines, flashing red lights, out-of-focus faces, gentle hands, softer voices, a distant siren, a brief, sharp glimpse of the inside of the ambulance, a frowning black face peering into my eyes.

Vaguely, I was aware of my body having been immobilized, my head wedged firmly in place so I couldn't move it from side to side. "What's the matter with me?" I said. "I can't move."

"Precautions, man. Just relax."

"How the hell do you expect me to relax? I can't move, goddammit."

But the face moved out of my field of vision. I lay there, staring at the inside of the ambulance.

They slid me out of the ambulance and wheeled me into the hospital. After what seemed like a very long time, the face of a very beautiful woman appeared over me. She had sleek black hair pulled back into a bun. It was streaked lightly with gray. "How do you feel?" she said.

"My head hurts. I can't feel anything in my arm."

"You've got a nasty bump." She touched my eyelid with her forefinger and shone a sharp dart of light into my pupil. She repeated the process in my other eye. "Can you tell me your name?"

"Yes, of course. Brady L. Coyne."

"What's nine times eight?"

"I always had trouble with the nines table."

She frowned impatiently. "Do you know who Larry Bird is?"

"Best damn basketball player on earth, that's who."

"Right. We'll forgive you the nines table. Do you feel nauseated, Mr. Coyne?"

"No. I told you. My head hurts." I tried to look directly

at her. I was still immobilized. "Why have they got me tied up like this?"

"You were complaining of numbness in your arm. We—"

"You think I broke my neck, right?"

She frowned. Her eyes were very dark, almost black. "That's a possibility. I'm going to do a few things. I want you to tell me what you feel."

She jabbed my toes, one at a time, with something sharp. I yelped ten times. She did the same with the fingers on my right hand. After a moment I asked her why she didn't test my left hand. She nodded. "I did."

"Oh, Jesus."

"It doesn't necessarily mean—"

"It means my neck's broken, doesn't it?"

"The only thing it means is that you've had a cervical injury. It's important that you remain immobilized until we know the extent of it. We're going to give you a shot. You'll sleep comfortably. Then we'll get X rays."

"My head?"

"No concussion." She placed a soft hand on my forehead. "You're going to be fine, Mr. Coyne."

She drifted out of my vision. I felt cool hands on me. Then the prick of a needle and a long, slow journey down a smooth slide into a black, dreamless sleep.

I woke up staring at the feet of two beds. They looked miles away. I closed one eye, and one of the beds disappeared. An animal in my stomach kicked once, and I managed to mumble, "Aw, shit," before I puked all over my chest. I found that I still couldn't move my head.

Almost instantaneously a woman in white materialized beside me. She frowned sympathetically and shook her head. "Demerol will do that," she said. She wiped my face with a damp cloth, stripped the blankets off me, and managed to replace them without moving me.

"I'm terribly thirsty," I croaked.

"Sorry. No water. We've got you on an IV. Water will upset your stomach."

"Please."

She smiled. She was dark and slim and quick-moving. She had a very long nose, which had once been broken. Her eyes were soft hazel and slightly uptilted at the corners. "No," she said. "Doctor's orders."

"Am I paralyzed? I can't move."

"You're in traction. You have a cervical injury."

"My neck's broken?"

"No. You'll be fine. The discs up here"—she touched the back of her own neck—"were damaged. You'll have to wear a collar for a while after you get out of traction. You'll probably have discomfort in your left arm and shoulder. Your vertebrae are pinching the nerves. That's all. The doctor will explain it all to you."

"My head?"

She touched my face and smoothed back my hair. "No fracture. No concussion. You were very lucky."

"Do you know what happened to me?"

She shrugged. "Nobody seems to know."

"There was a car . . ."

She patted my shoulder. "Just relax, Mr. Coyne. You're going to be fine. I've added a drip to your IV . . ."

I drifted into and out of sleep for what seemed like a long time. It was interrupted once by a very young male doctor who seemed more interested in examining a clipboard than me. He shone a penlight into my pupils, took my pulse, made notes onto the clipboard, and disappeared without ever speaking to me.

Later Charlie McDevitt came by. "Looks like the truck won," he said.

"Charlie, I feel absolutely shitty."

"They say you're okay."

"What do they know about it?"

He pulled up a chair beside me. "I thought of bringing you flowers. I thought of bringing you booze. I didn't bring you anything."

"All I want is an ice cube to suck on."

"Sorry, pal."

I fell asleep while he was talking to me.

The next time I opened my eyes, Charlie was chatting with Becca Katz down there about a hundred yards away at the foot of my bed. She was laughing. I figured Charlie had told her something intimate and embarrassing about me. After a minute my eyes focused and they didn't seem so far away.

"Hi," I said.

Becca came over. She bent and kissed me softly. "Ugh," she said. "Your lips are all chapped."

"All the better to eat you with, my dear."

She glanced over her shoulder to Charlie. "I think he's fine."

She sat gingerly on the foot of my bed. Charlie took the chair beside me. "What happened?" he said.

"Hit-and-run, I guess. I was on my way to the elevator. I remember hearing a car coming at me. I guess it got me."

"Nope," said Charlie. "The doctors say there's no evidence that you were hit. They figure you threw yourself out of the way and landed on your head. Damn awkward of you."

I squeezed my eyes shut, trying to remember it. "I heard glass break. I figured it was me and the headlight colliding."

"That was that big clunker of a briefcase you were carrying. It was smashed all to hell. Papers scattered all over the place."

"Then he got out of the car," I said, remembering. "I heard the door open and him walking toward me. Then a car started up somewhere else in the garage. It must've panicked him. He got back into his car and drove away. He was probably going to search my pockets. Or maybe—"

"Or maybe finish you off," said Charlie.

"Do you have to be so candid?" said Becca.

"Hayden," I said. "Same as Les. He probably thought he got me anyway. The car hitting the briefcase. He must've figured it was me."

"The same man who came to my house and hit me," said Becca. "He was after that film. I told him you had it. He figured, in the briefcase—"

"Hey," I said. "Don't blame yourself. Anyway, he didn't get anything. Gloria has it. It's all still there."

"He probably assumes he killed you, which serves his purpose just as well," said Charlie.

"Do you have to talk like that?" said Becca.

"So what do you figure he thinks is on that film?" said Charlie.

"There's nothing incriminating on it," I said.

"He doesn't know that," she said.

"All those pictures that didn't come out. Whatever they would've showed. That's what he's worried about." Becca's cheek was puffy and discolored. "How do *you* feel?" I said to her.

She smiled crookedly. "I'm fine. Ugly, but fine."

"I missed our date with Kerrigan today," I said.

"That was yesterday, actually." She reached down and squeezed my foot through the blankets. "I went. I took care of it all by myself. I came in to see you yesterday. Don't you remember?"

"No."

"You called me Gloria. You asked for your sons. I called her and told her what happened. She was here last evening, along with both boys. They seem to be fine young men. And I liked Gloria. I'm not sure she liked me."

"They were here?"

"Sure. We all had an interesting visit."

"What was I doing?"

"Sleeping. Moaning and groaning. Licking your lips. You have not been scintillating company."

"I don't remember any of that. Gloria and the boys being here."

"They've kept you pretty doped up. Anyway, you took quite a whack to the head," said Charlie. "Hopefully, you got some sense knocked into it."

"What worries me is what got knocked out of it."

The next time I woke up, my nurse was there fussing with my bedclothes.

"Hi, beautiful," I said.

"How are we feeling?"

"What day is it now?"

"Sunday."

I shut my eyes to calculate. Thursday night I had gone to Becca's. That was when she had been assaulted. Friday morning was when I had been run down. I had lain in the hospital all day Friday and all day Saturday. My memory of most of it was nil. "I've lost nearly three days out of my life."

"You're lucky, at that," she said. "Come on. We're going to dangle."

She moved behind me and fussed with the contraption that held my head immobile. Then she gently lifted my shoulders and strapped a soft collar around my neck. "Move slowly, now. I want you to sit up and turn around."

I obeyed. She was strong and confident as she helped me pivot around so that my legs hung over the side of the bed. I was momentarily dizzy. But she steadied me until it went away.

She helped me to stand. I leaned on her and shuffled a few steps. Then she steered me back to the bed. I found myself drenched in perspiration. I lay back on my pillow, exhausted.

"That was excellent, Brady. This afternoon we'll take a little walk."

"What's your name?"

"I'm Miss Perini."

"Miss?"

"Or Miz, if you prefer."

"But not Missus."

She smiled and shook her head.

"You're very beautiful."

She grinned. "Don't go getting any ideas."

"I'm feeling a little better."

"Yes. Horniness is usually a sign of that."

"Do you have a first name?"

"Of course I do."

"Will you tell me?"

"If you promise to call me Miss Perini in front of the doctors. Some of them are very stuffy that way."

"I promise."

"Denise. Dee to my friends."

I closed my eyes. "Thanks for everything, Dee."

"Don't go to sleep. There's someone waiting to see you."

"Maybe just a quick nap."

"No. I've brought you some ginger ale to sip. I've removed your IV. This noon you can eat."

"I'm not that hungry. But, yes, thirsty."

She gave me a glass with a bent straw. The ginger ale was warm and stale. It tasted great.

Dee Perini left the room. A minute later she returned, followed by a stocky woman with short, dark hair and a cute little uptilted nose. I stared at her, trying to sort out old data that seemed to have been misfiled in my brain.

"You," I said after a minute. "I know who you are."

She smiled. "I doubt it, Mr. Coyne."

"No, I recognize you."

"I'm Sharon Bell. I assure you we've never met."

I shook my head slowly. I found it painful so I stopped. "The pictures. You and Hayden. You're Derek Hayden's lover, for Christ's sake."

She smiled again. "No, I'm not Derek Hayden's lover."

"But the pictures . . ."

"There's a lot you don't know," she said. "Are you feeling well enough to talk? I was here yesterday but they said you were in no condition."

"Sure. Absolutely. Let's talk."

Dee Perini, who had been standing beside Sharon Bell, said, "Please try not to take too long." To me she said. "I'll be back in an hour or so. How does chicken broth sound to you?"

"Nothing I love better than chicken broth."

Dee left and Sharon Bell took the chair beside me. "Let me get right to it," she said. I tried to nod. The collar made it difficult. "I am a special investigator with the Securities and Exchange Commission, Mr. Coyne. That may surprise you.''

"Yes."

"About two months ago, we put together some numbers that caused us to begin asking questions about American Investments. I won't bore you with technicalities, but the upshot of it was that there seemed to be large sums of money moving in and out of their accounts that we couldn't account for. Dummy accounts. Action in foreign banks. Nonexistent investors. Profits we couldn't locate. The addition and subtraction didn't work.''

"What did you suspect?"

She shrugged. "Insider trading, possibly. Or laundering dirty money. Or some sort of scam. Using investors' funds as up-front money for something turning over big profits. Big, unreported, illegal profits, profits on which taxes were not paid. Oh, it was very sophisticated, and the data were tucked away in several dozen places, any one of which wouldn't really raise an eyebrow. We crunched a lot of numbers in our computers before we were confident enough to begin our investigation. And we started with no workable hypothesis.''

"Are you some kind of undercover agent?"

She laughed. "No, not really. I operate in a very straightforward way, usually. I go in, armed with the equivalent of a subpoena, and seize records. In this case, however, because the evidence was so sketchy, I did it a little differently. Based on some preliminary snooping around, I decided to approach one of the partners. Derek Hayden. I went to the office one day. He wasn't in. I wrote him a note and clipped my card to it. Invited him to lunch. He showed up.''

"I'm beginning to get the picture," I said.

She nodded. "I was prepared to lie a little, to offer veiled threats, to hint at bargaining and negotiation. You see, the way I figured it, the main man was the other partner, Arthur Concannon. Hayden wasn't lily-white, or course. But as I see it, he's sort of a gofer, a broker, an up-front man. The brains, the real crook, is Concannon. I said all this to Hayden, once I realized he would cave in easily.''

"So that's what all those clandestine meetings were about.''

"Yes. He agreed to feed me information.''

"So you could get the goods on Concannon.''

"Right. I guaranteed him immunity, which is what we often have to do. I met with him several times. Frankly, he didn't give me much. Not enough to move on. The last time I saw him, he was visibly upset. Claimed that Concannon was on to us. He was frightened.''

It all made abundant good sense to me. Concannon was the one who hired Les, using some woman who looked like Farah Fawcett to pose as Hayden's wife. Les got photos of Hayden and Sharon Bell. He thought they were having an affair, but in fact Hayden was slipping the SEC agent the goods on Concannon. First Les told Concannon's lady friend, posing as Hayden's wife, that Hayden was not fooling around. And he told Hayden that he had been hired to follow him. Then Les visited with me, and I persuaded him to come clean with his client. So he told the mystery woman that Hayden was, after all, engaged in an illicit relationship. Gave her the photos to prove it. She took them to Concannon.

The rest was fuzzy, but I figured it this way: Concannon decided he had to get rid of Hayden. Poor Les happened to be tailing Hayden at the time, armed with his long-lens camera. Maybe he actually tried to photograph Concannon murdering Hayden. None of those pictures came out. All he got was Hayden standing beside Concannon's car. But Concannon didn't know that. Concannon saw Les, followed him home, and ran him down. Then I visited him in his office, asking questions about Hayden. Concannon remembered Les's camera and appeared at Becca's house, clad in a ski mask. She told him I had the film. So he followed me home, or was waiting in my parking garage for me. Ran me down, too, interpreting the solid impact of his headlight against Les's briefcase as the splitting of my skull.

"Did you try to call Les's office?'' I said to Sharon.

She nodded. "Yes. Many, many times. That was you who answered, wasn't it?"

"Yes. How did you get on to Les?"

"Hayden told me about it. He said he bought the photos and that Katz burned the negatives. I asked him if he looked at the negatives, and he turned white. The man was very frightened."

"With good reason," I observed.

"Anyway," she said, "the next time I saw him was the night before he disappeared. The night before Katz was killed." She looked at me. "I've been doing some sleuthing since then. I've talked with the Somerville police, for example."

"Thus making the connection between Les's death and Hayden's," I said. "Concannon murdered both of them."

"We don't know for sure that Hayden's dead, of course," she said. "But, yes, that's the presumption. And that's how I heard of you. Which is why I'm here."

"To tell me all this?"

She nodded. "Among other things. I've pieced it together. Have you?"

Again I tried to move my head. I succeeded and regretted it instantly, as an arrow of pain shot down my left arm and lingered in my elbow and fingers.

"Are you all right?" She was frowning at me.

"I've got this pinched nerve. Gotta be careful." I hunched my shoulders and carefully shifted my position against my pillow. "I think Concannon killed both Hayden and Les. Hayden because he was going to expose their scam, and Les because he witnessed Hayden's murder. Then he beat up Becca and ran me down, looking for that film that he thinks shows him zapping Hayden. Concannon's our man."

"So," she said after a moment, "I'm wondering if you could help us."

"I am in no shape to help anybody. Besides, how do I know you are who you say you are? Maybe you really are Hayden's girlfriend. Maybe it really was Hayden who killed Les."

"I'm sorry." She unzipped her bag, which had been resting on her lap, and extracted a thin leather case. She handed it to me. I flipped it open. It contained her picture and an impressive card identifying her as Sharon Bell, Special Agent, Securities and Exchange Commission.

I gave it back to her. "Nice photo," I said.

"Think so?"

"Better than anything Les got of you. You are, of course, more beautiful in person."

"I am a very ordinary-looking woman, Mr. Coyne."

"I often find that ordinary-looking women are the most beautiful," I said. "Okay. I expect they'll let me out of here pretty soon. How do you want me to help?"

"I can't promise you it won't be dangerous."

I tried to shrug. I was having trouble expressing myself in body language. "I can't promise I won't chicken out when you tell me, either. But I'm willing to listen."

# 14

"You appear to be in some pain, sir," said Lucas as he led me through the upstairs bar to the back stairs of Barney's.

"I prefer to think of it as discomfort. It hurts less that way." The truth was, my neck felt as if it were filled with shards of broken glass, and my left arm ached with the dull persistence of an old war wound.

The doctor had instructed me to wear the collar all the time. I nodded when he said it, and he smiled at me. "You won't, I know. So you will suffer. Don't call me. There's nothing I can do for you. Whiplash injuries don't heal. Wear the neck brace and you'll feel better."

I didn't wear it, of course. I couldn't stand the idea of people staring at me.

The doctor also advised me to avoid tension-producing situations.

Lucas was an ancient black man, a vision of Uncle Remus, with round laughing cheeks and a fringe of cotton hair encircling his head. He had waited tables at Barney's for as long as I had been going there. Before that he had been a porter on the Boston and Maine.

The back stairs wound down to the cellar dining room, a long, narrow room without windows. Three walls were paneled with old barnboard. The other was brick. Photographs depicting scenes of Boston in the Gay Nineties hung here and there in simple black frames. Pale orange lights glowed dully from pewter sconces. The tables were aligned along one wall, widely separated from each other.

Barney's could be found only if you knew where to look, which was down a narrow alley off Boylston Street opposite the Common. It was favored by lawyers and Republicans for the privacy it guaranteed. Barney's was a prime battlefield for the civilized jousting and feinting of the political and legal warriors who battled there. At Barney's no one rushed patrons through a meal. Lawyers commonly spent entire afternoons there, huddling with clients or adversaries, plotting, conniving, giving and taking, advancing and retreating, until the law's work could be done. Waiters seemed to possess a sixth sense that enabled them to materialize tableside at the precise moment when a fresh martini was needed. We lawyers often showed up in midmorning and, allowing ourselves to be deceived by the perpetual dusk in the cellar dining room, began immediately to consume the offbeat variety of beers that Barney's specialized in. At some point, my adversary or I would ask for the Oysters Rockefeller. Later perhaps a bowl of the fresh fish chowder, washed down by a Reisling of Lucas's choice.

And much later we would stumble up those stairs, blink at the afternoon sunlight, and congratulate each other on a day's work well done.

It was a leisurely, discreet sort of place. It was very expensive.

It was where I chose to meet Arthur Concannon.

A few days after I was released from the hospital, I had gone to Concannon's office. Melanie Walther greeted me warmly, calling me by my first name. I was vaguely surprised that she remembered me. I asked if she had heard from Derek Hayden, and she shrugged and shook her head.

"I have something for Concannon," I told her.

"He's in his office, if you want to wait a minute."

"Don't bother him. Just give him this." I handed her a sealed envelope.

"Is that it?"

"It? What?"

"What you came here for?"

There was a mischievous query in her voice. I nodded. "Yes. That's it."

The note that was sealed inside the envelope said: "I am Lester and Rebecca Katz's attorney. I have a business proposition. If you would care to hear it, please meet me downstairs in Barney's at four Thursday afternoon. If you do not appear, I will take my business elsewhere." I stapled my business card to the note.

Lucas seated me at the table at the end of the room. "A beer, sir?"

"What is the beer du jour?"

"A nice dark from Israel. We serve it warm."

I rubbed my neck and grimaced. "I'll try it. Keep an eye out for my guest, please. I'm expecting him at four-thirty."

I had mentioned four in my note. I assumed he'd be late. He wouldn't want to appear too eager.

Lucas returned with my beer. It was bitter and heavy and I knew too many of them would set the steel drums to beating inside my head.

I wondered if Concannon would show up. My guess was that he wouldn't—unless he was as guilty as Sharon Bell deduced. If he had done all she thought—committed fiscal felonies, hired Les to follow his partner, killed said partner, killed Les Katz, beat up Becca, run me down—he might be unable to resist the bait I had trolled in front of him.

On the other hand, he might figure the best way to gain his end would be simpler: He might decide to try again to kill me.

At four-fifteen Lucas returned to my table. "Another, sir?"

"I didn't enjoy that one very much. I think I'll switch to my usual."

Lucas nodded. "A little heavy for my taste, too."

He was back in about a minute with a double shot of Jack Daniel's on ice with a side of branch water.

I sipped and smoked and tried not to play out scenarios. The truth was, I didn't know what I'd say to Concannon if he did show up. Sharon Bell had tried to coach me. But it made my head hurt and my neck ache. I told her that my doctor had instructed me to avoid tension and that I'd just have to play Concannon by ear. This did not seem to fill her with confidence. I didn't let on that it didn't inspire me, either.

It was close to five when I looked up to see Lucas leading Concannon along the length of the room toward my table. He stood beside me for a moment, looking uncertainly at me. I neither stood nor offered my hand. Finally he shrugged and sat across from me.

"Sir?" said Lucas. "Something to drink?"

"Bring him one of those beers," I said.

"I want Scotch," said Concannon. "Dewars. No ice, no water, no soda."

Lucas nodded and left. Concannon and I stared at each other until Lucas returned and placed a glass on the table in front of Concannon, who lifted it and allowed himself the tiniest of sips.

"Okay," he said. "Here I am. You probably find that enormously significant."

"I suppose I'd find your failure to appear significant, too."

He shrugged, sipped, and allowed his mouth to twitch in what I assumed was an expression of amusement. "You mentioned a business proposition. What is it?"

"I'm not very good at obfuscation and misdirection. Pussyfooting. Beating around bushes."

Concannon nodded. "Generally a waste of time."

"I've got those photos you want so bad. They're for sale." So much for Sharon Bell's coaching.

His expression didn't change. "Photos, Mr. Coyne?"

"The ones Les Katz took the night you killed him. The ones you beat up Becca and ran me down to get." I smiled. "Those photos."

His grin broadened. "I have a word of advice for you, Mr. Coyne."

"What?"

"Don't try to bullshit a bullshitter."

"Wouldn't think of it. This is the deal—"

Concannon held up a hand. "Before you make your pitch, I want you to know something. Okay?"

"Shoot."

"You are going to offer me some sort of bargain. I am neither going to accept nor reject it. I will wait until you're done. Then I will thank you for the drink and leave. You'll hear from me—if you hear from me at all—some other time. Satisfactory?"

I nodded. "Satisfactory."

He took a healthier swig of his Dewars and waved his hand. "Let's have it, then."

"Okay. Les got pictures. Becca gave the film to me. I got it developed. I know what's on it. It's what you wanted when you went to her house and when you ran me over later that night. Technically, the film belongs to Becca. She'd rather sell it than turn it over to the police. She asked me to try to arrange it." I hesitated.

"Continue," said Concannon.

"Twenty-five thousand dollars for the negatives and the prints. If the deal isn't made within one week, it all goes to the cops."

He nodded. "Twenty-five grand. One week."

"The film is in a safe place," I added. "If anything happens to me—"

"Sure, sure." He waved his hand as if a fly were bothering him. "Is that your pitch, Mr. Coyne?"

"That's it."

He studied me with what appeared to be mild amusement for a moment. He lifted his glass and drained it. Then he stood up. "In that case, thank you for the drink, Mr. Coyne," he said. And without offering me his hand, he turned and left.

I rubbed my neck. Avoid tension-producing situations, the doctor had said.

Lucas brought me another Jack Daniel's without being asked.

I stopped at a pay phone near the Park Street subway entrance. Using a pay phone was a precaution I thought unnecessary but that Sharon Bell had insisted on. She was staying at a fancy hotel in Brookline. I figured Uncle Sam would end up spending more on this operation than he could hope to recover by prosecuting an investment company. But justice, of course, has value beyond measure.

She answered on the first ring. "Bell," she said, businesslike.

"Coyne."

"How'd it go?"

"I couldn't tell."

"Did he go for it?"

"I couldn't tell that, either."

"So where does it stand?" She sounded impatient.

"Look," I said. "I offered him the deal. He neither accepted it nor rejected it. He's too smart for that. He didn't give himself away at all. He'll let me know within one week if he wants to buy the film."

"Or else he'll come after you."

"Yes. There is that possibility, as you seem to enjoy reminding me."

"I'm having second thoughts about having talked you into this."

"Thank you," I said. "I'm having second thoughts about allowing you to talk me into it. But it's too late to think about that now."

"Be careful. Please."

"I know. You've already got Les Katz's blood on your hands."

She was silent for a moment. "That's not entirely fair," she said finally. "But don't think I'm not fully aware of it. Did you tell Concannon you'd taken precautions?"

"Sure. I'm no hero. Actually, with all the film and stuff at my ex-wife's place, I'm wondering if there's any way Concannon could figure that out."

"Look," she said, "if you're worried—"

"Hell, of course I'm worried. But I figure, based on what we know of his style, his first move would normally be to beat the shit out of me. Hopefully, our little tête-à-tête this afternoon has preempted the necessity for that."

"Not necessarily."

"Right," I said.

"Brady, I really think—"

"I am not going to lug that gun around with me. It's uncomfortable. It makes my suits hang wrong."

"Yeah, I've noticed what a fashion plate you are."

"Look, Sharon. The last time I took that thing out of my safe, I ended up blowing a hole in a man's chest. He died."

"You told me. He was an evil man. You probably saved two lives by doing it."

"A moot point. I'll take my chances without the gun."

"I'd feel a lot better—"

"Your feelings, dear lady, have nothing to do with this. If you think I'm playing this charade out of patriotism, or some peculiar fondness for the Securities and Exchange Commission—or because you are a sexy wench—you're quite thoroughly mistaken. This is for me and Les Katz and Becca. This is personal. It happens that just now your needs and my drives intersect, so I'm cooperating with you. If I want to do it without a weapon, and without a bunch of agents shadowing me everywhere I go, then that's my choice."

She was quiet for a moment. Then I heard her chuckle. "A pretty speech, sir." A loud, rhythmic noise echoed in the telephone receiver. She was applauding.

"Sneer if you must," I said. "But look. I'm a careful person most of the time. This time I'm forewarned. I'm looking over my shoulder a lot. Anyway, I don't think Concannon wants to kill me. At least not right away. He might like to torture me some. It comforts me to think about it that way."

"You are a most peculiar man."

"Thank you," I said humbly.

She sighed. "So we wait."

"Yes. We wait for him to call."

"We hope he does call."

"Because if he doesn't, it means we have misjudged him."

"Or," she said, "it means I have misread the entire situation."

"Which would blemish your otherwise pristine record."

Another chuckle. "Exactly. Take care of yourself, Brady."

"Believe me, I intend to."

# 15

Two days passed with no word from Arthur Concannon. I used a pay phone each evening to report to Sharon Bell. She did not seem concerned. "He's checking you out," she said. "He's a cautious, careful man. He knows how to play these games. We've got to play better, that's all. Patience."

"What's he looking for?"

"A connection to me. He found out Hayden was meeting me, we assume. That's why we've got to be careful."

"Supposing he learned that you and I are in cahoots?"

"In cahoots!" she fairly roared. "Oh, my God. In cahoots, he says. You been watching *Gunsmoke* or *Bonanza* or something?"

"What's wrong with 'in cahoots'?"

"Nothing. It sounds like something you'd say, actually. Okay, so what if Concannon figured we were in, as you say, cahoots? I don't know. He still needs the film. It would certainly make him even more careful. And—"

"And more dangerous," I finished for her.

"Yes," she said quietly. "That's what I was going to say."

What I didn't tell Sharon Bell was that it contradicted my

nature to sit around waiting for the other guy's moves. It's what makes me a lousy chess player. The longer my opponent takes before he moves, the quicker I want to go. It's why I'm better at physical games than cerebral ones.

So the longer I had to wait for Concannon, the more I itched to do something.

I temporized by making a couple of phone calls. The first was to Kerrigan, the Somerville cop, whom I caught at the station just as he was going off duty.

"Do you remember me telling you about that Audi that was parked in the garage at the Alewife T station?" I said to him. "The one belonging to Derek Hayden?"

"Sure I remember."

"Whatever happened to it, do you know?"

"It's still right there. We ran it through the registry computer, verified it belongs to Hayden. Had the lab boys go over it inside and out. They found nothing special. Been hoping Hayden was going to show up, but so far no go. I tried to get the chief to stake it out, but he didn't feel we could swing it manpowerwise, given the thinness of our evidence that it was connected to a crime. I talked with the guys in the booths who take the money when you drive out. Promised them an easy twenty bucks if the Audi with the license plate TARZ pulled up to the window and they stalled him and called me within two minutes. They work eight-hour shifts, different guys on weekends, one spare for sickouts—seven contacts I made. None of 'em has called me yet. At this point, I figure Hayden's Audi is a dead end. I was back there a few days ago, matter of fact. It was still there, collecting dust and a big fee."

"It's still there because Hayden is probably dead," I said, and I proceeded to tell him how Sharon Bell and the Securities and Exchange Commission figured into the picture, and that Les Katz had probably been killed because he witnessed Hayden's murder.

"I just had this awful thought," said Kerrigan.

"I've been having my share recently."

"I wonder if the lab guys prybarred open the trunk of that Audi."

"You said you were there recently."

"Yeah."

"Did you get out of your cruiser?"

"Sure. Wanted to see if there were any smudges on the dust."

"Smell anything?"

He laughed thinly. "No. And we've had some warm days lately, too. Okay. Scratch that idea. It's a relief, I admit."

"You going to continue to spy on the Audi?"

"Not much sense, I guess. Assuming Hayden is dead."

"I assume he is."

"I suppose I ought to call his wife, then, tell her she can come and pick it up," said Kerrigan.

"If you don't mind, I'd like to take care of that. I want to talk to her anyway."

"You're kind of a nosy son of a bitch, aren't you?"

"Les Katz was a friend of mine," I said. "You don't mind, do you?"

"Nah. Good luck to you. I'm going home, get my supper."

The other phone call I made was to a state cop named Horowitz, who owed me a minor favor. When his switchboard put me through to him, he growled, "Yeah, Horowitz."

"Dear, dear," I said. "Did we arise from the wrong side of the bed this morning? Do we have a hair across our ass?"

"Who the hell is this?"

"Coyne."

I heard him pop his ever-present bubble gum. "Okay. So hello, all that shit. Whaddya want?"

"Come on, Horowitz. Be nice. You owe me."

He sighed. "I beg your humble pardon, sir. In what way may I be of service?"

"Better. That is much better."

"Don't push it, Coyne."

"Sorry," I said quickly. "I'd like to give you a chance to discharge your debt."

"It's been keeping me awake nights. You have no idea." He paused. "You mean, then I wouldn't have to be polite to you?"

"Absolutely. You could be your normal unpleasant self."

"And we'd be even?"

"Right."

"So what is it?"

"I just want to know if a certain person has been reported missing."

"State?"

"Huh?"

"Jesus," he muttered. "Where's this person from, for Christ's sake?"

"Oh. Harvard. The town. Harvard, Massachusetts."

"And that's it?"

"You need his Social Security number?"

"No. I mean, if I tell you this person's on my missing list, we're even?"

"Right."

"Okay. Good. What's his name?"

"Hayden. First name of Derek." I spelled it for him.

"Hang on. Lemme punch it up on my little computer here . . ."

In the time it took me to fish a Winston out of a pack, light it, and take one drag, Horowitz was back on the phone. "Yep. Hayden, Derek. Reported missing by his wife, Brenda Hayden, on January fifteen. Last seen January six. There's some other stuff here. Want it?"

"Like what?"

"What he was wearing, physical description, automobile registration, presumed destination, like that."

"I don't need any of that. Thanks. The slate is hereby wiped clean. Tabula rasa, my friend."

"What do you want this for?" said Horowitz.

"You don't want to know."

"And why the hell not?"

"Because if I told you, then you'd owe me again."

He suggested I perform a maneuver that sounded uncomfortable. Then he hung up.

Still no call from Concannon. I waited at my office well past my normal closing time, growing itchier by the minute. Julie poked her head in at five-thirty. "I'm out of here," she announced.

"I think I'll hang around for a while," I said. "Lots of heavy legal matters to attend to."

"Ho, ho."

"Don't both with the answering machine," I called after her. "I'll turn it on when I go."

I took the ceremonial bottle of Jack Daniel's from its hiding place in the file cabinet and poured myself three fingers. Three adult male fingers. I lit a cigarette and swiveled around to study the night lights of my city. Many people find elevated views of cities at night beautiful. I'm a moon and stars man, myself. You can't see moon and stars very well from the city. You can see them very well from the wilderness, though, and if God's natural lights are doubled by their reflection in a placid Maine lake, so much the better. And the hoot of an owl, the wail of a loon, or the pinkletink of a spring peeper will elevate my soul infinitely quicker and higher than the honks and curses of congested city traffic.

I've come to recognize that I'm an anachronism, a country boy doing the work of a city lawyer.

I'm an anachronism in several other ways, too. Becca Katz and Gloria Coyne could attest to that.

I stubbed out the cigarette half smoked, drained the glass, and grabbed my coat. I had to do something.

I took only one wrong turn before I found the Hayden place in Harvard. I pulled in behind Brenda Hayden's Volvo and sat there for a minute, regretting my impulsiveness. It was downright rude to drop in without at least phoning first.

On the other hand, my intentions were pure.

Warm orange light seeped from the back windows of the farmhouse into trapezoid-shaped puddles on the snow-covered lawn. Frozen slush crackled under my feet as I mounted the back steps onto the open porch. I rapped on the door and waited, blowing open-mouthed into my hands and rubbing them together. Overhead the sky was an inverted black bowl studded with a million beautiful points of light. My breath came in foggy puffs. Radiational cooling, the meteorologists called it. It was a cold night, and it would get colder.

I waited three or four minutes before the door opened. Brenda Hayden stood there frowning. She was wearing baggy bibbed overalls over a flannel shirt. She was taller than I remembered.

"Brady Coyne," I said loudly through the storm door. "Remember?"

She nodded vigorously and opened the door.

"Hi," she said. "A surprise. Come on in. Crawl up to the woodstove. It's beastly out there."

I entered, stomped my feet on the mat inside the door, and shook my jacket off. She took it from me and draped it over the back of a chair.

"Have a seat. Let me clear off the table."

She removed the dirty dishes from the kitchen table and stacked them beside the sink. "Nice to see you again," she said casually, as if I visited her regularly. "How've you been?"

"I'm fine. I'm sorry to drop in like this—"

"But you just happened to be in the neighborhood." She laughed. "Hey. Nobody just happens to be in this neighborhood. Look, want some coffee or something? A drink?"

"Whatever you're having."

"Coffee, then. It's all fresh and hot."

She turned to the coffeepot, grateful, it seemed to me, to have something to occupy her. Her movements were quick and nervous, which seemed natural enough given the suddenness of my appearance.

She slid a mug of coffee in front of me. "Black, right?"

"I'm flattered you remembered."

She shrugged and sat across from me. She flicked a hank

of hair away from her forehead with her forefinger. She stared into her mug for a minute, and then, without looking up, she said, "No, to answer your question, I have neither seen nor heard from Derek. I reported him missing the same day you suggested I should. It's become—I'm not handling it as well as I thought I would."

"I'm afraid I don't have any news, either," I said. "Except I located the Audi, and you can pick it up if you want."

"Where is it?"

"In the Alewife parking garage."

She nodded and sipped her coffee. "I suppose I'll fetch it sometime. I keep thinking I should leave it there for when Derek comes back. Anyway, I've got my brother's Volvo, so there's no big rush. I bet the parking fee will be astronomical."

"That's not your car out there?"

"No. My brother Andy's planning to sell it. Meanwhile he's letting me use it. I suppose if I ask him he'll drive in with me to get the Audi." She hugged herself and frowned at me. "Mr. Coyne—"

"Brady."

"Brady. Why did you come here?"

"Do you mind if I smoke?"

"If you have to smoke, that means you have bad news for me, right?"

I lit a Winston. "I told you. I don't have news of any kind. But I have some suspicions, and I figured no one else would be telling you what's going on. It occurred to me that you have a right to know."

"I'm not sure I want to know."

"Where are your children?"

She rolled her eyes and smiled. "With my mother. It's just been too weird around here. I've been too weird, is what I mean. Mother lives in Ayer. That's just the next town over. Where Andy lives. Good old Mom drives the girls to school. She's been oh, so very understanding. She assumes Derek has run off with some busty young thing. She wants to tell me that she knew it would happen all the time, but she hasn't quite screwed up her courage yet. So she just looks at me mournfully and says consoling things. Which only serve to upset me.'' She arched her eyebrows at me. ''Is that it? Is that what you came to tell me?''

''That he's run off with some busty young thing?'' I shook my head. ''No. That's what I originally thought. But now . . .'' I let my voice trail off, reluctant to say it.

She leaned across the table to me. ''Now you think he's dead, don't you.''

I nodded.

She stared at me for a moment. Then abruptly she stood up. She went to the sink and began to rinse off the dishes and stack them in the dishwasher, keeping her back to me. I remained sitting at the table, watching her. When she was finished, she poured some detergent into the machine, slammed it shut, poked a button, and it began to hum. Then she turned to face me. I somehow expected that she'd been weeping. But her eyes were dry and her face composed.

''Okay,'' she said, a harsh edge to her voice. ''Why don't you tell me who you really are and why you're really here.''

I lifted my palms and let them fall. ''I'm Brady Coyne, I'm a lawyer, and I'm here because I'm involved in an investigation that, in part, includes trying to find your husband.''

She wiped her hands on the seat of her overalls and came back to the table. She sat across from me, laced her fingers together in front of her, and said, ''After you left here the last time, I got to thinking. This tall man with gray eyes, who says he's a lawyer but dresses like a lumberjack, he comes and starts pumping me for information about Derek, and, like a dummy, I cry and spill out my guts, and after he leaves I suddenly realize I don't even know why he came here, unless it was to get me to spill out my guts. He tells me nothing except for some double-talk about me presumably hiring some private investigator. Then I said, what the hell, he's a lawyer and that's how lawyers do it, and he seemed nice enough, so I sort of forgot about it. Then he shows up again. Now I want to know. What the hell do you want out of me?''

I tried to smile ingratiatingly. It felt stiff. "For one thing, I wanted to tell you about the Audi."

She nodded skeptically. "You could have called."

"And I wanted to know if you'd heard from your husband."

"And *I* want to know why you care."

I nodded. "Okay. Fair enough. When I was here the first time, I thought your husband ran over a friend of mine and killed him. This friend had taken photos of him. I figured the photos were incriminating in some way, and that's why Les was killed. My friend was a private investigator. I thought you hired him. I thought—"

"You thought Derek was having an affair. I remember that. So what's different now?"

"I've learned some more things. Now I don't think it happened that way. Now I think your husband's partner, Arthur Concannon, may have killed my friend."

Brenda Hayden smiled crookedly. "And Derek, too. Is that it?"

I nodded. "That's how it looks."

"So you came here to—what?—to prepare me for the possibility that my husband is dead?"

"Partly. But mostly to see if there was anything you could remember he might've said about Concannon—business deals, financial transactions he might've been worried about, something personal, maybe, something about the man he was afraid of. Or maybe a hint of mistrust." I shrugged. "Anything you could think of."

She stared at me for an instant before she allowed her eyes to shift away from my face. She studied something beyond my right shoulder for a long time before she spoke. "Arthur Concannon," she said carefully, spacing out her words, "is my friend. Our friend. He and Derek are partners and friends. They are not in competition with each other. They are not enemies. I don't know what you're talking about."

"That's a pretty speech, Brenda," I said. "Just the right mixture of indignation and sincerity. But it took you too long to polish it. Tell me the truth."

She snorted, a quick, harsh laugh. "And just who the hell do you think you are, barging into my house with accusations and suppositions and horrible ideas, telling me my husband has been murdered by his best friend and business partner? All this talk. I don't know what any of it means. Goddamn it, anyway. Goddamn you."

She pounded on the table with both of her clenched fists. Then the tears came, although the fury on her face did not diminish. She wiped her cheeks with quick angry swipes of her wrists. "Oh, it pisses me off when a man makes me cry," she said. "I see you sitting there, saying to yourself how you're so tough, you can make a weak female person bawl. Listen, Mr. Lawyer. I am angry and I am frustrated and that's why I'm crying, so don't you try to take any credit for it."

"Look, Brenda—"

"No. You look. Look for your jacket and look for the door and look for your God damn car and get the hell out of my house."

I shrugged. I slipped into my jacket. I opened the back door, paused, and said, "Thanks for the coffee, anyway."

I closed the door behind me quickly, before I could hear her retort.

I sat in my BMW for several minutes before I started it up, trying to sort out the impressions and random messages that were pecking at the outer fringes of what passed for my mind.

Brenda Hayden's performance had been good but flawed. I didn't know her well enough to be certain, but she struck me as a little off-center. Eccentric. Her reactions seemed too studied, her emotions too calculatedly hysterical.

On the other hand, she had been missing her husband for three weeks. I told her I thought he was dead. How else should she react?

I turned the key in the ignition and flicked on the headlights of my car. Before I backed out of the Hayden driveway, I jotted down the license number of Brenda Hayden's brother's Volvo.

What I especially wondered about, as I drove the unlit

country roads of Harvard, Massachusetts, was this: Why had there been two sets of dirty dishes on Brenda Hayden's kitchen table when I arrived? Would a woman be likely to brew a full pot of coffee for her own after-supper consumption?

And what was the significance of the five pieces of unmatched luggage I had seen lined up in the hallway that led into her living room?

# 16

---

When my clock radio clicked on at four o'clock, I was already wide-eyed and waiting for it. The morning man announced the weather with more good cheer than seemed warranted—clear and cold in the morning, clouding over, with snow beginning in the afternoon. Accumulations of six to twelve inches in the Greater Boston area. Double that west of Route 495. Blowing and drifting.

The temperature in Kenmore Square was seven degrees. The sun would rise at six thirty-three.

I wanted to be there at least a half hour before that.

Before bed the night before I had laid out what I'd be needing—my faithful old red flannel long johns, wool pants, two pairs of wool socks, Herman Survivor boots, a heavy wool turtleneck sweater, ski mittens, and my insulated camouflage duck-hunting jumpsuit.

I tugged on the long johns and went into the kitchen. I filled my steel Stanley thermos with scalding water from the tap to heat it up while the coffee brewed. My Smith and Wesson .38 was loaded and waiting on the table. Sharon Bell would be gratified. There was also a box of cartridges and my 10X German binoculars.

I gobbled down two stale doughnuts and a big chunk of extra-sharp Vermont cheddar. A breakfast to stick to the ribs. Then I dumped the hot water out of the thermos and filled it with coffee. As an afterthought I added a hefty shot of bourbon. Then I finished dressing.

I tucked an unopened pack of Winstons into one pocket, the revolver and spare cartridges into another, slung the binoculars around my neck, and waddled out to the elevator. I hoped none of my neighbors would see me.

Less than an hour later I turned into a little side road about a mile from the Hayden farm in Harvard. I left my BMW parked against the plowed snowbank. I hoped it wouldn't attract attention for the few hours I expected to be gone.

The woods that extended from the little roadway to the edge of the Hayden property were thickly overgrown and hilly, and in places the powdery snow, sheltered from the melting rays of the sun, came to my knees, so that even in the frigid predawn air I sweated copiously under my heavy clothing. I blessed my wool underwear, which possessed the miraculous quality of insulating and warming even when wet.

The setup was as I pictured it, based on my one daylight visit to Brenda Hayden. The thick woods ended abruptly halfway down a hillside, which stretched the rest of the way as an open field for about a hundred yards to the farmhouse. I could see the back door of the house, the barn, and the Volvo parked in the driveway. The far side of the house and barn were sheltered by a dense clump of spruces. In the distance, Mount Wachusett humped into the horizon, a gray-purple lump in the thin yellow light.

I hunkered down among a clump of pin oaks that still held most of their sere leaves, adjusting my back against the trunk of a larger oak so I had a clear view of the Hayden farmyard. I focused the binoculars so I could clearly read the license plate of the Volvo.

When I had arrived home the previous night after my visit with Brenda Hayden, I dug out the computer list of license numbers Charlie McDevitt had procured for me. The numbers I had copied down from the Volvo matched the registration of someone named Andrew Bayles, who lived at 129 Center Street in Ayer. Andy, brother of Brenda.

I wondered if Brenda herself had been driving the night Les Katz snapped the photos of Derek, the night Les had been run down and killed. Or if, for some reason, Arthur Concannon had been driving the Volvo.

I wondered who had eaten supper with Brenda before I got there. I wondered where she was planning to go, and for how long, with her five suitcases.

I felt edgy, the way I felt before a courtroom appearance, the same way I used to feel before a big ball game. I patted the Smith and Wesson, which hung heavily but comfortingly in my pocket. I'd objected to lugging the weapon on a well-thought-out abstract principle. I decided to carry it for a very practical reason.

I didn't know what I expected to observe from my hillside blind. But whatever it was, I knew I wanted to see it. So I crouched on the edge of the woods and watched the sky brighten as the sun rose somewhere behind me. Spread before me was a scene Andrew Wyeth might have painted—a sleepy farmyard, a row of gaunt, leafless sugar maples, fields and meadows bumping away toward distant hills, woodlots bordered by stone walls, brushstrokes of burnt umber and ochre washed in the sharply angled yellow-orange light of the newly risen sun. A lone crow cruised and flapped overhead. Somewhere a dog barked once. The sky evolved imperceptibly from gray to cold, pale blue. Another bright winter's day.

I poured a mug of coffee from the thermos and held it awkwardly in my mittened paw. The coffee scalded my tongue when I sipped it. The afterburn of the bourbon lit a small, welcome ember in my stomach.

The silver Mercedes pulled in behind the Volvo a few minutes after seven. I shifted my position to gain a better view and discovered my left arm aching and my neck stiff. The doctor had told me the disc damage in my neck was permanent. I still didn't want to believe him.

A man in a navy blue topcoat and felt hat stepped out of the Mercedes. I trained my binoculars on him. It was Arthur Concannon, which didn't surprise me. It was one of the scenarios I had played with after I began to suspect that Brenda Hayden was entertaining company. The oldest motive for murder in the world was lust for a friend's wife.

Concannon chunked the car door shut, paused to blow into his cupped hands, and went around to the passenger side. He opened the door and bent to help a woman slide out. Through the binoculars I could see that she wore spike heels and a calf-length green dress under her fur coat. She had a spectacular tumble of long blond hair—very much in the style of Farrah Fawcett.

This was the mystery woman, the one who had told Les Katz she was Derek Hayden's wife when she hired him to spy on Hayden.

She turned to reach into the car for something, and in that instant I saw her face. Melanie Walther, in a wig.

She retrieved her purse and, holding on to Concannon's arm, went to the back door of the Hayden farmhouse. After a minute the door opened and Concannon and Melanie Walther went inside.

I adjusted my back against the oak tree and tried to make sense out of what I had just observed. Okay, so Concannon was a friend of the Haydens and was disposed to comfort Brenda in her time of confusion over the disappearance of her husband. Nothing wrong with that. Perhaps their friendship had evolved into a relationship more intimate. Natural enough. No crime in that, either.

But why visit at seven in the morning? And why bring Melanie along in her Farrah Fawcett wig? And what about those suitcases?

I calculated quickly. It would take me fifteen minutes to tromp back to my car through the woods. If Concannon should begin to tote Brenda's luggage out of the house and stack it in the trunk of his Mercedes, I'd have time to get

- **158** -

back to my car and follow them. I suspected they'd head for Logan International Airport. It would satisfy my curiosity, if nothing else, to learn their destination. If I were clever, I might be able to persuade a ticket seller to tell me if they were flying on round-trip tickets, and if so, when they were expected to return.

I had no idea what good any of that information would do. But I would relate it to Sharon Bell. She'd know how to use it.

In spite of my clothing, my inability to move around was increasingly causing me to suffer from the cold. My toes were already numb. I made fists inside my mittens to try to restore circulation to my fingers.

I poured another mug of coffee and cradled its warmth in my bare hands as I sipped it. Nothing seemed to be happening below me. I decided to risk a cigarette, even though I knew it would contract the capillaries in my extremities and accelerate the effects of the cold. I had never been one to pay much attention to such details.

The smoke burned harshly in my lungs. I doused the butt in the snow, half smoked, and huddled there miserably. For all I knew, Concannon and Melanie were planning to spend a leisurely day visiting Brenda, in which case I had every reason to expect to end up as a piece of ice sculpture by the evening.

My coffee was gone and I was beginning to shiver inside my long johns when the black Lincoln pulled into the driveway. I checked my watch. Eight-thirty. I fumbled for the binoculars that hung around my neck. My hands obeyed reluctantly. They felt like hunks of wood.

When I focused on the face of the man who climbed out the passenger side of the Lincoln, a new warmth suffused my body.

He wore a gray topcoat that looked several sizes too large for him. He was bareheaded, revealing a dramatic thatch of snow-white hair. His deeply lined face, his grand beak of a nose, that big outsized head perched atop the emaciated body, the giant cigar clenched between his teeth—all belonged to

Vincent Tremali of Providence, Rhode Island. That face, cigar and all, had snarled from the cover of *Time* magazine six months earlier. "Underworld Kingpin Takes the Fifth" was the lead story's headline for that issue. Every afternoon for four weeks Vincent Tremali's surprisingly deep, well-modulated voice had growled, "No comment" to the bevies of television reporters who accosted him, while behind the heavy doors of the Federal District Court a grand jury fumed in helpless frustration.

Their first prize witness failed to appear to give testimony, and while it was rumored that a man of his general description was seen lounging on the beach in St. Maarten at about that time, his identity was never confirmed.

The second prize witness was found in the basement of an abandoned warehouse in Holyoke, Massachusetts, tied to a chair, with a single bullet hole in the back of his neck.

The third, fourth, and fifth prize witnesses pleaded failed memory. Threats of contempt citations failed to stimulate them.

The sixth prize witness offered testimony that reddened the face of the prosecuting attorney. A subsequent perjury charge did not persuade the dapper young man to alter his view of the truth.

Observers reported that Vincent Tremali, when his turn finally came, was calm, almost regal in his aloof response to the badgering of federal prosecutors. He chose to exercise his constitutional rights as an American citizen. He sounded more like John Barrymore than Marlon Brando. And he continued to assert that right as the lawyers played a game of tag team with him for four weeks, bombarding him with questions about loan-sharking, prostitution, toxic waste contracts, numbers, dope, extortion, arson, and just about every other form of criminal activity imaginable.

After a while the cartoonists and pundits began to depict the United States government as the bad guy. Tremali became a kind of perverse folk hero.

It was, most agreed, a magnificent performance by a seasoned pro, and Vincent Tremali was reluctantly excused by the grand jury. Indictments were not forthcoming.

This shriveled-up little guy was probably the most powerful man on the East Coast. He was now standing in Derek Hayden's farmyard in Harvard, Massachusetts, at eight-thirty in the morning, hunching his shoulders against the frigid air, puffing his cigar, and looking around the property as if he were a prospective buyer.

From the driver's side of the Lincoln emerged a second man, approximately twice the size of Tremali. This guy wore a plaid sport coat over a white turtleneck. He was constructed like an offensive tackle. I found his face in the binoculars. He, too, looked familiar, although I couldn't recall his name. One of the prize witnesses whose memory had repeatedly failed him.

As I watched, Tremali spoke to his driver, who went to the back door of the farmhouse. He hit the door with the side of his fist. The door opened halfway for a moment. Then it closed and Tremali's driver returned to the Lincoln. The two hoods stood there stamping their feet for a couple of minutes. Then Tremali leaned close to his driver, who nodded, opened the door of the Lincoln on the driver's side, and hit the horn. The loud, sudden honk struck me as a violation of the pastoral silence of the farmyard. A moment later Arthur Concannon hurried out of the farmhouse, buttoning up his topcoat as he hastened, hand outstretched, to greet Vincent Tremali. I was disappointed that the two men did not kiss each other on both cheeks.

Their breaths came in little puffs as they stood by the Lincoln and talked. Tremali's cigar bobbed as he spoke. The big driver stood deferentially aside, looking away as if intent on studying the woods where I hid, the snow-blanketed meadows, and the spectacular distant views of Mount Wachusett.

After conferring with Concannon for a couple of minutes, Tremali removed his cigar from his mouth and gestured with it to his driver. The big man opened the trunk of the Lincoln, reached in, and pulled out a large suitcase. He lugged it to Concannon's Mercedes and set it heavily down on the icy driveway. Then Concannon opened the trunk of his car and wrestled the suitcase into it.

The driver got back to the Lincoln. Concannon and Tremali talked for another few minutes, their heads close together. Tremali seemed to be doing most of the talking. Concannon kept nodding. From my vantage point a little more than a hundred yards distant, I could hear the low murmur of their voices. I could not make out any of their words.

Finally Concannon and Tremali shook hands. Concannon opened the door of the Lincoln and held Tremali's elbow as the old man climbed in. The Lincoln backed out of the driveway and crept away at a sedate pace.

Concannon remained standing in the driveway until the Lincoln disappeared from sight. I held my binoculars on him and saw his private smile before he turned and went back into the house.

I glanced at my watch. The entire transaction had taken less than ten minutes.

I shivered. I was cold. I was also struck with the realization that I seemed to have stumbled onto something way out of my league. I had no desire to become involved in anything remotely related to Vincent Tremali. The newspaper descriptions of the witness with the bullet hole in the back of his neck remained vivid in my mind. He had deep cigar burns on his face and neck. His bare toes were sodden, bloody pulps. The papers speculated that someone had smashed them, one by one, with the round end of a ball peen hammer.

I had been hidden in that copse of pin oaks for a little more than three hours. I doubted if the temperature had yet made it to double figures. The chill had penetrated to my kidneys. I realized I had to give serious thought to hypothermia.

I fumbled for my binoculars and thermos. I looked forward to turning on the heater in my BMW. I would skedaddle back to Boston. Then I'd tell Sharon Bell what I'd seen and leave it on her lap. I was ready to devote my full attention to the divorce settlements and estate plans of my loyal clients, and leave the Concannons and Tremalis of the world to the proper authorities.

I was out of my league. I was proud of myself for acknowl-
edging it, for once.

The voice that came from behind me was soft and polite.
"Don't bother turning around, my friend. Place both hands
behind your head, if you don't mind terribly," it said.

"Ah, shit," I said as I obeyed.

# 17

He approached me from behind, patted my pockets, and removed my revolver.

"My, my," he said, chuckling. "A weapon. And what, my good man, are you doing?"

I still hadn't seen his face. I had never head his voice before. Yet I thought I knew who he was.

"Deer hunting," I said. "I'm looking for deer."

"This is private property, and the deer season has been closed for two months. You are in serious trouble."

"I'll leave. I'm sorry."

He chuckled again. "I'm afraid it's not that simple. Why don't you stand up now."

It was awkward. I was stiff and numb. I hoisted myself to my feet and turned. At his side the man held a lever-action rifle pointed at my navel. It looked like a .30/30, the kind of gun cowboys always carried, short-barreled and deadly. He was tall, with a thin face and a high forehead. He wore dark-rimmed glasses. He was smiling good-naturedly.

"You know me, don't you?" he said.

"I suppose I do. Derek Hayden."

He bowed politely. "At your service. And you, of course, have to be the ubiquitous Mr. Coyne."

"The same. How—?"

"Did I find you? Not that difficult. Vincent Tremali is a careful man. Your automobile was observed. Your footprints in the snow. Freshly made. They went away from the car and did not appear to return. Rather a primitive exercise in logic to conclude that the creator of those footprints was still lurking in the forest. Which Mr. Tremali reported to us. I went out the back door, around behind the trees, and lo, here we are."

"I'm not breaking any law," I said.

"Deer hunting with a pistol indeed," he said, pretending to enjoy the joke. "They said you had a bit of a wit about you. Why don't you come to the house and join us for hot chocolate."

"Aw, thanks just the same, but I think I'll get going—"

"Let's go," he said, in a decidedly less friendly tone. He gestured with his rifle, and I began to slog through the snow, down the slope. "Keep your hands behind your head," said Hayden. "If you don't mind."

"I do mind. I feel like a prisoner of war."

This amused him. "Yes. Well put. That is approximately what you are, Mr. Coyne. A prisoner of war. Very apt."

I stumbled several times in the deep snow. My legs responded tardily to the instructions my brain was barking at them. By the time we arrived at the back door of the Hayden farmhouse, I was once again drenched in perspiration.

A warm blast of air greeted me inside the kitchen. Arthur Concannon, Melanie Walther, and Brenda Hayden were seated around the table, sipping from mugs. Melanie, I noticed, had removed her blond wig.

"Greetings, greetings," said Concannon heartily, smiling and gesturing for me to take an empty chair at the table. "Join us, please. Cocoa for Mr. Coyne."

I sat. "Do you mind if I remove a few layers of clothing?" I said.

"Slowly. Carefully," said Hayden.

I stepped out of the jumpsuit and shrugged off the heavy sweater. Then I bent and unlaced my boots.

Brenda Hayden placed a mug in front of me. I looked up at her. "Thanks, Brenda," I said.

She avoided meeting my eyes.

Hayden remained standing, leaning carelessly back against the wall, his .30/30 slung under his arm. Concannon, Brenda, Melanie, and I were seated at the table. A cozy little suburban gathering on a crisp winter's morning.

Concannon leaned toward me. "What brings you around, Mr. Coyne?"

I shrugged. "Couldn't sleep. I love these winter days, you know? Wondered if I might spot some deer in the fields."

Concannon's mouth smile remained fixed. His eyes glittered dangerously. "No bullshit," he said softly. "Remember? Now tell me. I want to know what you know."

I have always admired the men in television melodramas who, strapped into the electric chair, offered wisecracks before the death jolt. I envied those who chose to make eye contact with their firing squad, refusing the blindfold. I valued a particular image of myself. I didn't want to be a man who shit his pants before he died.

I figured I had nothing to lose by telling Concannon what I knew. It would be better than sniveling and groveling. Maybe it would put him in the mood to talk to me, although I was hard-pressed to see how that would help.

"What I know is this," I said. "I know you guys are mixed up with Vincent Tremali. I know who and what he is, which gives me an idea of what and who you might be. I know Tremali just delivered a heavy suitcase to you. I know Derek here, has been talking with an agent from the Securities and Exchange Commission—"

Concannon's head snapped around to glare at Hayden. "Is this true?" he hissed.

"Now, wait a minute, Arthur—"

"Shut up."

"But you asked—"

"I got my answer." Concannon turned back to me. "Go ahead, Mr. Coyne," he said softly. "Tell me more."

"I know that one of you ran down and killed a friend of mine. I know that one of you beat up Becca Katz, another friend of mine. I know that one of you tried to run me down, too. I know I have some interesting photographs that Les Katz took. I know that if something should happen to me—"

Concannon raised his hand imperiously. "Enough," he said. "No bullshit, remember?" He stared at me. I returned his gaze steadily. I hoped I looked calmer than I felt. "Okay, then Mr. Coyne," he said. "Let's hear the rest of it."

I shrugged. "That's what I know." I emphasized the word "know."

"So what do you think, then?"

I looked around at the faces of the people in that room. Hayden's finger was resting on the trigger of his rifle. He was staring at me, his eyes narrowed behind his glasses. Melanie Walther and Brenda Hayden were studiously gazing out the kitchen window toward the barn out back.

"I think I'd like some more cocoa," I said.

Concannon jerked his head at Brenda. She hopped up as if she had been bitten by a snake. She took my mug, refilled it from a saucepan on the stove, and placed it in front of me. I sipped from it.

"This is what I think," I began. "I have told most of it to Sharon Bell, who is heading up the team of investigators from the SEC. They are on to you guys. You are laundering money for Vincent Tremali. They may not know that yet, but they're pretty close. Sharon Bell approached Hayden, here. She knew he was the weak one. They met a number of times. You," I said, thrusting my chin at Concannon, "must've suspected something. You had Melanie dress up like Farrah Fawcett, pose as Mrs. Hayden, and hire my friend Les Katz to follow Derek. Les saw him meet Sharon Bell. Took photos of them. Then, for reasons peculiar to himself, Les lied when he talked to Melanie and told her that Hayden was clean. He also approached Derek with what he thought was evidence of his marital indiscretions. In any case, he continued to follow Hayden after that. He stumbled onto a transaction. Took more photos. It's all on film. I've seen it." This was a lie, but I didn't see how it could hurt. "You guys," I went on, gesturing at Concannon and Hayden, "spotted Les. One of you followed him and ran him over outside his house. I'd guess it was Hayden. How'm I doing so far?"

Concannon had been staring at Hayden. Now he slowly turned his head to look at me. "You're doing just fine, Mr. Coyne. Why don't you keep going."

I shrugged. "After you killed Les, Hayden hopped a plane. Where do you do your business? Switzerland?"

"Nassau," said Concannon.

"Whatever," I said. "By the time Hayden returned, I had already showed up at your office and had visited Brenda. So you decided it would be a good idea for Derek to lay low. I thought you had killed him."

Concannon smiled. He twisted his head around and spoke over his shoulder to Hayden. "Derek," he said, "let me see that gun for a second."

Hayden frowned and passed the rifle to Concannon. Concannon held it in his hands as if he were examining it. Then he pushed himself back from the table and stood up. With the rifle he gestured to Hayden. "Derek, have a seat."

"Now, just a minute, Arthur."

"Sit!" commanded Concannon.

Hayden looked at him, then at Brenda and Melanie, as if asking for their help. They looked away. Hayden shook his head back and forth. With a small shrug of his shoulders, he sat in the seat Concannon had vacated.

Concannon spoke to me. "I should have killed him," he said conversationally. "If I had known about the SEC broad I would have."

"I told her nothing," said Hayden quickly. "Honest to God, Arthur. I was putting her off the track. It was working out. If it hadn't been for that Katz following us that night—"

"Shut up." Concannon's voice was weary. "I don't want to hear about it."

"But we shouldn't even be discussing this with him here," said Hayden, jerking his head at me.

"Oh, that won't matter." Concannon smiled pleasantly at me. "You understand, of course, Mr. Coyne."

I nodded. "Sure. Win a few, lose a few."

"I like your spirit. Too bad we didn't meet each other a long time ago."

"Pity," I said. "Can I ask a couple of questions?"

Concannon spread his arms magnanimously. "Be my guest."

"How do you do it? What you do for Tremali, I mean."

"Oh, it's really a model of simplicity, Mr. Coyne. Very efficient, very profitable. If I do say so myself. Vincent, of course, manages a number of extremely lucrative businesses. Some are perfectly legitimate. Others—well, I suspect you can figure that out."

"You really shouldn't—" began Hayden.

Concannon turned to him. "Derek, please. Mr. Coyne and I are having an intelligent discussion. I'm certain it will be way over your head. You are excellent at the limited responsibilities I have assigned you. But don't bother trying to make sense out of the sophisticated stuff Mr. Coyne and I are chatting about."

"I'm in it as deep as you," said Hayden, sulking.

"You are in a good deal deeper, my friend." Concannon turned back to me. "Where was I?"

"You were telling me what an astute businessman Vincent Tremali is."

"Of course. His, ah, enterprises are doing extremely well. Especially those that involve cash transactions. Some time ago Vincent found himself unable to cleanse all that cash through his legitimate operations."

"When the grand jury was after him."

Concannon nodded.

"So he turned to you."

He bowed. "Yes. I have several numbered accounts in

– 169 –

Nassau banks. As secure and discreet as those in Switzerland, and a good deal more accessible. And the nature of my business allows us to deposit large sums in our numbered accounts and write checks on those accounts to deposit in the various investment accounts our business holds. Our clients like it. They have reaped consistently generous growth in their investments. Vincent Tremali likes it. And,'' he added, grinning broadly, ''I like it.''

''You couldn't do it without me,'' said Hayden.

''That, my dear friend, is where you are wrong. You are a donkey. A mule. Strong back, weak brain. I load you up, shoo you onto an airplane. The thing about you, Derek, you look legitimate. And you can follow directions.'' He shook his head sadly. ''I didn't know you were that stupid, though.''

''I'm telling you, she got nothing out of me.''

''Immaterial, actually. It was a matter of time. I'm certain she's brighter than you. She would have got what she wanted. Your mistake was not telling me the instant she approached you. Now, I'm afraid, you have lost my trust. Without my trust, Derek, you have nothing.''

''I killed that guy for you. Doesn't that mean something?''

''Too little, too late, as it turns out.'' Concannon turned back to me. ''Impressive, what?''

He wanted my approval, for what reason I couldn't determine. I decided to play along. ''Ingenious. I'm very impressed. Tremali's business must have been worth a lot to you.''

''A lot? Mr. Coyne, right now in the trunk of my Mercedes there rests a suitcase full of money. It is tightly packed. It is very heavy. Nearly two million dollars. Ten percent of that money is mine. We have made several trips on behalf of Vincent Tremali. He is very happy with our work.''

''As well he might be,'' I murmured. ''So today you're off to Nassau, eh?''

''Well, our plans may have to be altered slightly. Originally Derek and I and Melanie and Brenda were going to take a little vacation. We were going to hire a schooner and cruise for a while. Your recent, ah, intrusions had suggested that we might make a more lengthy trip of it. A week or two, perhaps a month. Now''—he opened his hands as if he were a magician about to release a dove—"I'm afraid we're going to have to adjust those plans.''

"We get rid of Coyne and we're clear,'' said Hayden eagerly.

Concannon shook his head sadly. "Not that simple, I'm afraid.'' He glanced at his wristwatch. "My goodness. It's nearly ten-thirty. Time does have a way of fleeting when one is engaged in stimulating conversation. Our plane leaves at—what, Melanie, dear?''

She fumbled in her pocketbook and removed a sheaf of airline tickets. "Two-ten,'' she said. Those were the first words she had spoken since I had come into the room. I realized that Brenda had said nothing at all. I wondered how the two women were involved.

"Well, then,'' Concannon said, "we must get moving. Did you have any further questions, Mr. Coyne?''

"How are the ladies tied up in this?''

Concannon gazed fondly at Melanie and then at Brenda. "Both of these lovely ladies, Mr. Coyne, are in love with me. And, of course, I with them. I consider myself a fortunate man.''

I smiled. "In that single respect, I consider you a fortunate man, too.''

Hayden had placed the Smith and Wesson .38 he had taken from me on the counter beside the sink. Concannon's gaze fell upon it. He took it in his left hand and expertly checked to see if the cylinder was fully loaded. Then he leaned the .30/30 against the wall. He gestured at me with my pistol. "Stand up, Mr. Coyne. Lace on those boots. We're going outside.''

I thought of lowering my head and taking a run at him. I thought of tipping over the table and diving for the rifle. I thought of speaking to an imaginary person standing behind Arthur Concannon.

I thought of a bullet zipping through my chest. I bent and laced up my boots.

"Now you," said Concannon.

Hayden lifted his head. "Me?"

Concannon smiled and nodded. "You."

Hayden looked from Brenda to Melanie. Neither met his gaze. He shrugged and stood.

"Out the door, you two," said Concannon. "Slowly and carefully, now. The least I can do for you is make it quick and painless. I know you agree. Open the door please, Derek."

Hayden obeyed.

"Now," said Concannon, "put your hands on top of your head." When Hayden did that, Concannon said to me, "Now, Mr. Coyne, place your hands on Derek's shoulders. And, gentlemen, if any one of those four hands moves, I shall not hesitate to shoot you both."

So Hayden and I stood there foolishly, waiting for Concannon's next command.

Brenda and Melanie remained seated at the table, watching us, with no expression showing on their faces. I wondered how I could have misjudged them so badly.

"Ta, ta, ladies," said Concannon. "We'll be but a few minutes. Perhaps you could carry Brenda's luggage to the car while you're waiting. In a few hours we shall bask in tropical paradise, sipping exotic rum drinks, frolicking on the white beaches. I have purchased new swimwear for both of you. I know we will all enjoy it."

Concannon marched Hayden and me outdoors. He paused to squint up at the sky. The air had begun to thicken, carrying with it the unmistakable smell of an imminent snowfall. The thin gray cloud cover lay like a wet tarp over the rural scene. The sun was a fuzzy yellow blotch above it. Concannon nodded and allowed himself a small smile.

He directed us into the barn. Inside the doorway, he ordered us to stop. "Over there," he said, gesturing with my gun at a row of garden tools that leaned against the inside wall. "Each of you. Pick up a shovel."

We obeyed. As we bent close together, Hayden whispered to me, "Let's take a whack at him."

"Not me, pal," I said.

"He's going to make us dig our own graves, for Christ's sake."

"Ground's frozen. I doubt it."

I turned to face Concannon, holding a long-handled spade. Concannon kept himself beyond range of a swipe. "Okay. Good," he said. "Now, Mr. Coyne, you resume your position behind Derek. That's it. Now I want each of you to put those shovels across the small of your backs and hook your elbows around them. Yes, good. That's it. Now, men, forward, march."

From that position, converting the shovels into weapons would be awkward and slow. So I marched behind Derek Hayden across the yard to the rear corner of the farmhouse. About fifty feet from the house we came to a roughly rectangular spot where the snow cover was visibly thinner.

"Stop here," said Concannon. "Now, boys, dig."

Hayden and I bent to the task. "This is the septic tank," Hayden hissed to me. "The bastard's going to dump us in there."

We shoveled off the snow. The ground on top of the tank was soft. Less than two feet down my spade hit something solid, and within fifteen minutes we had scraped the earth off the top of what looked like a two-thousand gallon septic tank. There were two concrete lids on it, each slightly less than two feet in diameter.

"Take the tops off," said Concannon.

They were heavy and wedged on tightly. Hayden and I worked together and finally managed to pry up an edge, slide our shovels under, and lever the top off.

The odor that burst out of that hole made me gag. I backed reflexively away. I noticed Hayden had reacted similarly.

Concannon's scheme became clear. I could find no flaw in it. He would kill Hayden and me and stuff our corpses into that godawful, stinking pool of septic waste. Then he would replace the top and shovel the earth back over it. He'd smooth the snow over that and fill in our footprints as he went back to the house. Six to twelve inches of new snow, the weatherman had predicted—probably significantly more than that, since Harvard lay west of the imaginary snow line of Route 495. Enough to hide all traces of what had been done.

Concannon and his ladies would fly away to Nassau. Hayden and I would soon be consumed by the hungry bacteria in our hellish tomb. Our bones would sink to the bottom. And who would look there for our bodies? Hayden had been a missing person for weeks already. The search was off for him. And what of me? Concannon would instruct Melanie or Brenda to drive my BMW to a parking garage or shopping mall near the airport. Nobody knew I had driven to Harvard. Nobody would look for me there.

The hopelessness of my situation became suddenly apparent. I had only one thought: Kill me quick. Don't—dear God, don't, please don't leave me to drown in that foul tank.

"Now the other lid," said Concannon amiably, standing, I noticed, out of range of the awful stench.

With bile rising in my throat I bent beside Hayden. He was muttering under his breath. Suddenly he yelled, "Now!" and in one swift motion he leaped sideways and swiped with his shovel at Concannon.

Concannon took one calm step backward, lifted the pistol, and pumped three quick shots into Hayden's chest. Hayden's body jumped backward, as if it had been rammed by a truck. He sprawled face up, arms and legs spread, onto the snow. A red stain spread out under him.

"Too bad," said Concannon. "I was going to shoot him in the back of the head. It would've been a whole lot neater. Ah, well. Now, sir, I'm afraid you are going to have to tuck poor Derek into the hole."

I was staring down at Hayden's body. "Jesus Christ," I muttered.

"Get cracking, Mr. Coyne. I'm running short of time here."

Numbly, I bent to Hayden's body. It was limp and awkward, and he had been a big man. I tugged at his arm. I could barely budge him. I started to stand up. "I can't—"

"Mr. Coyne, this saddens me, but I am out of patience."
Concannon raised the pistol and pointed it at my chest.

I stared into his eyes. Face the executioner. If nothing else,
Arthur Concannon would see my eyes in his sleep for the
rest of his life.

I saw the concussion of the bullet a barely perceptible
instant before I heard the report of the rifle. A white puckered
hole materialized on the side of Arthur Concannon's neck.
As I watched, the hole turned pink. Then blood welled up
in it and began to spurt from it as Concannon's heart pumped
his life out onto the snow.

He stood there for what seemed like a long time, frowning. He dropped the pistol onto the snow. In slow motion,
he reached up to touch his wound. Then he removed his hand
and held it in front of his face. The hand dripped with his
blood. Then he looked at me, and in the instant before his
eyes rolled up and he sagged to the ground, I thought I detected the beginnings of a smile in them.

I knelt beside Concannon and felt under his jaw for a pulse.
It was there, flickering dimly. Then it fluttered like butterfly
wings, and Concannon groaned quietly. Then he died.

I looked wildly around. Bracing herself against the side of
the house was Brenda Hayden. The .30/30 was trained on
me. Melanie Walther stood behind her. Both ladies looked
calm, composed.

I waved at them. "My God, thank you," I called.

They started to move toward me. I reached for the pistol
that Concannon had dropped. Brenda shouted, "No! Leave
it!"

I shrugged and stood to wait for them.

Brenda held the rifle at her side. She handled it comfortably. The two women came over and stood beside me. They
gazed down at the two dead men. Melanie shoved at each of
them with the toe of her boot. "They're dead," she said.

"Good," said Brenda. She knelt beside the sprawled
corpse of her husband. She touched his cheek tenderly, her
head bowed as if in prayer. She muttered. "Ah, Tarz . . ."

Then she stood up. "He was a bastard," she said to no one in particular.

"They both were," said Melanie.

"Well," I said, "that was good work. Helluva shot. He was about to—"

Brenda took a step backward. She held the stock of the .30/30 tight into her armpit. Her finger was on the trigger. The rifle was aimed at me.

"Hey, you can put that thing away," I said. "You got the bad guys."

The muzzle did not waver. "Come on," said Brenda. "Let's go back to the house."

I turned and started to walk. "You know," I said over my shoulder, "I'm getting a little tired of being paraded around at gunpoint. We've got to phone the police, you know. You saved my life. You're heroes."

We went back into the kitchen. I sat at the table without being told. I suddenly felt weak-legged and dizzy.

"Whew," I breathed. "I'm a little shaky. You going to call the police now?"

Brenda and Melanie exchanged glances. "You're a pretty nice guy, Brady," said Melanie. "We decided that while you were outside. At first we figured, let Arthur kill you both. Then we said, Brady's a reasonable person, and kinda sexy in a chauvinist sort of way. Anyhow, he's not really involved in all this, and it would be a waste. At least we ought to give him a chance. You do want a chance, don't you?"

I nodded enthusiastically. "You betcha. I do want a chance."

They both smiled. They had me by the balls and they were enjoying it. "Here's the deal," said Melanie. "Brenda and I are going to leave. You're going to stay. You can stay here and continue breathing if you'll do it our way."

"What's your way?"

She reached into her pocket and took out a small plastic bottle. She opened it and shook three tiny tablets into her hand. "This is a large dose. It will wipe you out for a while. But it won't kill you. I want you to swallow these."

"How do I know it won't kill me?"

She glanced meaningfully at the rifle Brenda held. "If it were lethal, it's still preferable, don't you think?"

I sighed deeply. "Yes, but it's really not necessary."

She smiled. "It won't kill you. Honest."

"Can I ask you something?"

"Sure," said Melanie.

"Were you two a part of this?"

"What do you mean?" said Brenda.

"I mean, when I came here the first time, you seemed genuinely concerned for your husband. You said you didn't know what could've happened to him, and I believed you. And you," I said, turning to Melanie, "when I went to the office that time it was the same. But now I see you here, ready to flee the country with these two guys, obviously partners."

"It wasn't like that," said Brenda. "I had no idea what was happening. Until a couple of days ago, that is."

"When Derek showed up."

"Yes. He said he was hiding. In his own house, for Pete's sake. Even then, I really didn't understand. Until this morning."

"Same here," Melanie said. "Oh, Arthur had me dress up in that dumb wig and pretend to be Brenda. He said it was a practical joke. You think I knew how American Investments made its money? I was a secretary. They never told me anything. All I know is that Arthur liked to buy me things. We had some fun. This trip we were supposed to be going on—a holiday, that's all." She rattled the pills in the palm of her hand. "So Brenda and I are going on a holiday anyway. After you take your pills."

"It's really not necessary," I said. "I think it's neat, what you're doing. A tidy sort of justice. You don't have to give me sleeping pills."

She handed them to me. "Swallow them."

I popped them into my mouth, tucked them into my cheek, and made a big show of swallowing. Brenda and Melanie smiled at me. "Now," said Brenda, "swallow the pills, please."

I started to protest, but the tablets had begun to dissolve in my mouth, and their bitterness activated my salivary glands. I had an urgent impulse to swallow, which I finally obeyed. I felt the pills slide down.

I leaned back in my chair. We all had some more cocoa. Brenda and Melanie kept watching me. I started to tell them about what had happened to Les Katz. I found myself repeating the phrase. "Les was a good guy. A good guy." I forgot what I was going to say next.

"You might want to curl up on the sofa," said Melanie, extending her hand toward me. I reached for it. My arm felt heavy and limp. It seemed miles long. I saw her smile, a beautiful, kind smile. An angel, I thought. Then her face split into two faces, and each of them split again, as if I were looking into a trick mirror. All of her faces were smiling as they receded into a fuzzy gray. . . .

It was dark when I woke up the first time. Early, I thought vaguely. My thoughts were clouds, and when I tried to focus on one of them, it dissolved into an opaque wisp. I seemed to keep waking up early. My clock radio. Soon it would click on. No. Something else. I let the clouds billow in. I'd just roll over until the radio went on.

The next time I awakened, sharp lights flashed in my brain. My head hurt, a dull, persistent ache behind my eyes. I needed aspirin. Bad hangover. What had I drunk?

It came back to me then, not all at once, but in disconnected images. Arthur Concannon gazing in wonderment at the blood that dripped from his hand onto the snow. The awful stink of that septic tank. Vincent Tremali's shrewd, immoral face. Derek Hayden's awkwardly sprawled body. The thwang of a rifle shot.

I was lying on a sofa in the Hayden living room where, I assumed, Melanie Walther and Brenda Hayden had deposited me. I was entangled in the crocheted afghan they had spread over me.

The house was dark and empty. I knew without looking that it was late. Somewhere a clock tick-tocked. A tree branch scratched against a windowpane.

I sat up to test my equilibrium. In that position, my head hurt a little more. But I was not dizzy.

It was 3:25 A.M. by the luminous dial of my wristwatch. Melanie and Brenda were long gone. They were in Nassau, now, sharing a suitcase full of cash. The more I thought about it, the better I liked it. Vincent Tremali's filthy money was being enjoyed by two lovely women who had, by virtue of working for and living with a pair of scumbags like Arthur Concannon and Derek Hayden, truly deserved it.

I fumbled in the darkness until I found a light switch. Then I went into the kitchen. The woodstove was cold and dead.

I tried three drawers before I found a flashlight. I recovered my boots, which Melanie and Brenda had thoughtfully removed for me, pulled them on, humped into my camouflage jumpsuit, and went outside.

The night was moonless, the air palpably moist. Snow as fine and hard as birdshot came angling down on a sharp northeasterly wind.

I bowed my head into the wind and trudged across the yard through the snow. Already the old tracks had been filled in and smoothed over.

The odor of the septic tank insulted the sweet country air. By the beam of the flashlight, I found the snow-shrouded lumps, the bodies of Arthur Concannon and Derek Hayden. They had not moved. Not one centimeter. Seeing them was an affirmation. I had imagined nothing. They were dead. And I was alive. I felt exultant. I had the urge to cry. I sensed no conflict in this.

I turned and walked slowly back to the house. I shucked off my boots, crawled out of the jumpsuit, lay on the sofa, and pulled the afghan over me.

Sleep came instantly.

# 18

Becca held up a tarnished silver bowl. "Wedding present," she said. "We got four of these." She wrapped it in newspaper and deposited it in a cardboard box. "Les said the only thing they were good for was wedding presents, and that we should save them for when we were invited to weddings."

"You're really leaving then," I said.

"I am really leaving. There's a little private school outside Philadelphia that needs an English teacher. Anyway, I've got to get away from here."

She climbed back up onto the stool and peered into a cabinet. She was wearing a baggy sweatshirt and baggy jeans with an orange bandanna around her hair. "Besides," she said without turning around, "you're not available, remember?"

I said nothing.

She handed down a china teapot to me. "Wrap this in a newspaper and stick it in the box, will you?"

I took the teapot in both hands. "Will you be okay?"

"I think so," she said. "Have they left you alone yet?"

"Finally. I think."

When I woke up from the drug-aided sleep in the Hayden farmhouse the morning after Arthur Concannon and Derek Hayden were killed, I phoned Detective Horowitz of the State Police. That initiated several days of off-and-on interrogation. Horowitz was candid with me. I was a suspect. He even recited Miranda to me, and I congratulated him on getting it right. I exercised my right to secure counsel and called Zerk Garrett, who expressed unbounded glee at the prospect of defending me in a criminal proceeding.

Ballistics confirmed that the Smith and Wesson .38 revolver licensed to me had fired the bullets that were extracted from Derek Hayden's chest. The absence of fingerprints on the rifle that had probably been used to kill Arthur Concannon (the bullet that passed entirely through his neck was never recovered) was attributed to my foresight in wiping the weapon clean.

Horowitz frowned frequently when I tried to explain what had happened. When I asked him what he thought my motive was, he said, "You tell me," as if he expected me to. He asked difficult questions. Zerk encouraged me to answer them. So what was I doing at the Hayden place with my car parked on a side road a mile and a half away? Why did I bring my weapon? Why did I wait almost twenty-four hours before reporting what I had allegedly seen? How well did I know Brenda Hayden? What exactly was my relationship with Melanie Walther? What was my connection with Vincent Tremali? What was in that suitcase?

Over and over again. When Horowitz got exasperated with me, a guy named Brescia took his place. Brescia had a soft voice and a polite manner. He was very persistent.

Zerk sat there through it all, one leg hooked over the other, grinning.

At my insistence, Horowitz talked with Sharon Bell. He remained skeptical, although I noted that his line of questioning moved in some new directions.

It wasn't until Melanie Walther and Brenda Hayden flew

into Logan and were greeted by a pair of burly state troopers that Horowitz and Brescia began to soften.

"They confirm your version of the shootings," Horowitz told me, popping his Bazooka. "Of course, they claim to know nothing about a suitcase full of money."

"I never said it was full of money," I said. "I didn't actually see what was in it."

"The women say they never heard of Tremali except on television. No suitcase full of anything, as far as they're concerned."

I shrugged. "I've only tried to tell you what I saw."

Horowitz grinned. "It's doubtful that Tremali is going to report a theft. It's doubtful that Miz Walther or Mrs. Hayden are going to claim a suitcase full of money on their ten-forties. Nassau banks do not communicate with the IRS. These broads may just get away with it."

"What about the shootings, then?" I asked.

"They tell it your way. Walther admits she shot Concannon. She saved your life. Hayden confirms it exactly. I'm not inclined to prosecute."

"Good," I said. I loved it. The two women were going to pull it off.

"Or you either," said Horowitz. "As much as I'd enjoy it, I guess we haven't got a case against you."

Zerk feigned disappointment. "My big chance," he moaned. "I was gonna finally make it. the black F. Lee Bailey. They woulda written my biography."

When I tried to pay him for his services, he muttered something about *Gideon v. Wainwright* and said he felt an ethical obligation to perform pro bono work now and then. "For certain destitute clients, you understand," he added.

I reminded him that I was familiar with the *Gideon* decision. I had tutored him on it before he took his bar exam.

Becca climbed down from the stool. "That's about it, I guess," she said. "The movers'll be here in the morning. Thanks for your help. For all of it."

"Just doing my job."

"Your job." She grinned slyly. "Does that normally include sleeping with the wives of your deceased clients?"

"Oh, sure. Absolutely. That's one of the main parts of the job."

"Well, I hope Les paid you enough."

"I have been handsomely rewarded."

"What exactly was your fee for this?"

"Ten bucks."

She smirked. "Okay, so you won't tell me."

"My fees," I proclaimed huffily, "are a private matter. Between me and my clients."

"Ten dollars!" She laughed. "You know, I wouldn't put it past you. Or Les. Les was as tight with a dollar as you are generous."

"Shows how well you knew him," I said. "Or me."

"So," she said. She held out her hand.

I took it. We shook formally. "Be well, Becca."

"I will miss you, Brady Coyne."


Irv Barth was happy. His estranged wife, Edna, was happy. Edna's attorney was happy.

I, therefore, was happy.

How does a couple, married twenty-two years and hell-bent on divorce, agree on the custody of what they love the most, when they both want to keep all of it?

It's hard enough with kids. It can be even harder, I've learned, with vacation homes and luxury yachts and golden retrievers. But it's pure hell when the dispute involves a priceless collection of American Indian artifacts that the couple, both archaeologists, have gathered over the course of a quarter century of expeditions. They were a team. They co-authored books.

As Julie said, the foundations of their marriage had been a shaky structure of flaked and chipped flint and obsidian. And it had collapsed underneath them.

The solution was fairly obvious, once we all got past the greed. I found a small museum in Palo Alto that was willing to turn over an entire room to the collection. It would be the Barth Collection, housed in the Barth Room.

Irv and Edna would reap a tidy tax write-off. They could visit their arrowheads and pottery shards whenever they wanted. They could add to the collection. Each would deliver an annual address at the museum—Irv in October, Edna in May—for which they would be paid handsome honorariums.

It worked out well. Only a reconciliation would have been better.

So I leaned back in my desk chair, laced my hands behind my head, swiveled around to gaze westward over the tops of the Copley Square buildings at the pink late-winter afternoon sky. Somewhere beyond the rooftops and chimneys there was a snow-covered meadow. My mind's eyes saw it clearly. The black serpentine shape that wound through it was the shell of ice that had frozen and thawed a dozen times during the winter over the deep-running brook that flowed under it. Native brook trout were finning drowsily in its currents. Pussy willows along the banks were feeling their sap begin to rise.

So was I. Spring was imminent.

I became aware of a buzz. I twirled around and picked up the phone. "Hi, Julie."

"You daydreaming again?"

"I was deep in thought. Arcane points of law."

"I bet. I've been buzzing you for about ten minutes."

"Surely you exaggerate."

"Gloria is on the line."

"Thank you." I pushed the button. "Hi, hon," I said.

"What's with the music?"

"Huh?"

"While I sat here on hold," said Gloria, "cobwebs forming on me, I was forced to listen to the Ray Conniff Singers perform a medley from *The Sound of Music*. You must remember how much I hate Julie Andrews."

"That music is a new feature designed for the listening enjoyment of the clients of my busy legal practice."

"I would have expected Buddy Holly or Chuck Berry. The Beach Boys, at the very least."

"Our music was selected on the basis of exhaustive research. The Ray Conniff Singers make people receptive to paying hideous fees to lawyers. What's up?"

"Last time you were here you left your gloves."

"And you suspect a Freudian accident."

"I suspect you continue to be scatterbrained."

"That was over a month ago."

"Billy's been wearing them," she said. "Want 'em back?"

"Billy can have them." I paused. "Is that why you called?"

"That's it. I've been meaning to. Keep forgetting."

"Are you all right?"

"I am terrific," said Gloria. She sounded sincere.

"Actually," I said, "I've been thinking about you. Had this crazy idea. What about lunch? We could hit the Iruña in Harvard Square. Say next Tuesday around noon?"

She hesitated. "I don't think I can make it."

"Oh." I cleared my throat. "So how's your lawyer friend?"

"He's fine, thank you."

"Still seeing him, then?"

"Yep."

"Oh, well, Perhaps we can do the lunch another time."

"Perhaps," she said. "Another time."